About the Author

Lucy Hawkins is a writer and artist who lives in Australia's Yarra Valley with her husband and two young daughters. She studied Journalism at the University of the Arts in London and worked at Cosmopolitan Magazine and The London Paper in the UK as well as newspapers and magazines around the world. Her original artwork, prints and homewares are sold in stores across Australia.

The Salvager's Quest

Lucy Hawkins

The Salvager's Quest

Olympia Publishers
London

www.olympiapublishers.com
OLYMPIA PAPERBACK EDITION

A CIP catalogue record for this title is
available from the British Library.

ISBN: 978-1-80439-174-7

This is a work of fiction.
Names, characters, places and incidents originate from the writer's
imagination. Any resemblance to actual persons, living or dead, is
purely coincidental.

First Published in 2023

Olympia Publishers
Tallis House
2 Tallis Street
London
EC4Y 0AB

Printed in Great Britain

Dedication

To my daughters, Josephine and Georgina.

Acknowledgements

Thank you to my husband, James, my parents, Heather and Richard and my mother and father-in-law, Mary and John, for your unwavering belief and support.

Chapter One

It was a hot summer's night in Healesville, a small town in Australia where two sisters, Stella and Dot, lived with their parents and a pet rabbit that raced around the living room and ate the curtains.

It was past the girls' bedtime and they were supposed to be asleep, but instead nine year old Dot sat on her bed while her twelve year old sister Stella, laid out items from her doctor's bag. Stella wanted to be a vet and so she practised bandaging things whenever she could. No one in the Peters' household was ever quite sure what they'd find under all the bandaged objects lying around the house and Mrs Peters wished she didn't have to unwrap so many things just to find her car keys.

This evening, as many evenings before, it was Dot's turn to be bandaged. Stella held one end of the gauze against her little sister's forehead and started wrapping it around and around her head, squashing her dark, curly hair onto her face and into her eyes.

'I can't see!' said Dot.

'I know, dear. You've had a nasty accident,' replied Stella in her doctor's voice.

'Can't I have a nasty accident on my arm for once? It's really dark in here. And hot and tickly.'

Stella sighed. Sometimes it was really exhausting being an amazing vet. 'Okay fine, a nasty accident on your arm.

Maybe two arms and a leg?'

'Deal,' said Dot, who was used to haggling with her sister but was not getting any better at it.

Stella unravelled the bandage and Dot yawned and rubbed her eyes. Stella felt sorry for her; maybe this patient could wait until the morning.

When she had put everything back in her doctor's bag, Stella looked at her sleeping sister, whose gangly legs were about to fall out of the bed, and nipped across the room to stick them back in. Then she changed into her matching PJ's and hopped into her own bed where she fell asleep thinking about how frustrating it was that she still hadn't caught and bandaged the rabbit.

Teddies rolled off beds as the girls tossed and turned. The clock in their bedroom ticked, their fairy lights blinked. Stella and Dot were awoken by a thud on the roof.

'What was that?' asked Dot, sitting bolt upright in her bed, her dark hair so knotted in her sleep that curls stuck out at every angle.

'I don't know,' replied Stella, her own mess of blond curls also behaving very badly indeed. 'It was too big to be a possum.' Her alarm clock said 11.13 p.m. The house was quiet and all was dark. She opened their bedroom window to have a look.

Nothing stirred in the garden except for the sound of the crickets.

But then the girls heard what sounded like a bird…talking! It went something like this: 'Squawk, hurry up, bok bok bok, tweet' and it came from the roof.

The girls climbed out of the window and onto the rose-covered trellis, something that they did often to look at the stars. But this evening as the girls peered over the gutter, they gasped at an extraordinary sight – a huge wooden ship sat on rubber cushions, a tall mast leading firstly to a crow's nest and then a giant hot air balloon!

'Bok bok bok...' said the strangest bird they'd ever seen. He had the body of a brown chicken, a black neck, a multi-coloured beak and a chicken's red comb on top of his head. 'Good evening! Stella and Dot, I presume?' squawked the bird.

The girls gulped in unison. The balloon started to deflate.

'My name is Gus, a pleasure to meet you.'

The girls looked at each other and back at the odd, talking bird.

'Word of your many good deeds and kindness to animals has reached Planet Beatrice. As a result, the Council believe you two are exactly what's needed to save the animals.'

'Save what animals?' asked Stella. 'And what is Planet Beatrice?'

'Beatrice is a most beautiful planet, slightly to the left of Pluto. It's a sanctuary for animals that are in danger of becoming extinct. The Council will explain further when we arrive. Actually, we really should be leaving quite soon. May I help you aboard?' And with that, the little bird extended a wing.

'Okay!' said Dot without hesitating.

'Umm, no!' Stella could think of a million reasons why this might not be okay. 'Are you crazy? Mum would kill us! That is if the dodgy ship doesn't first.'

'I can assure you it's expertly crafted...' said the

strange bird as the girls continued to argue.

'He says it's expertly crafted!' said Dot earnestly.

'You don't even know what that means.'

'Yes I do! It means there's a huge ship with a hot air balloon that's managed to fly from another planet and land on our roof. I'd say that's quite impressive.'

'I'm going to get Mum and Dad.'

'Oh no dear girl, I'm sorry. No Grownups must know, it would endanger all of the animals.'

'You see! I thought you want to save animals? It is literally the only thing you talk about,' pleaded Dot. Stella watched her wiggle her nose and move her eyebrows up and down and knew she was trying not to cry.

In truth, Stella was still a bit cross with her parents for not letting her keep a tiger snake she'd found yesterday.

'Of course I want to help animals!' She sighed and looked at Gus. 'You're going into space? Don't you need a rocket?'

'Oh no, they take too long and bits fall off them. Very messy.'

'So, just how long would this trip take? We'd have to be back before Mum and Dad get up.'

'I promise you dear girls, the ship is extremely fast. You'll be back before breakfast.'

Stella tended not to trust things straight away. She'd got a magician's box for Christmas a few years ago and knew all the tricks. But for some strange reason she just trusted this funny-looking little bird; she felt she had to go with him.

'All right then,' she said, smiling. 'Let's go.'

'Yippee!' said Dot and nearly fell off the roof.

14

'Ugh. Be careful!' Stella rolled her eyes, grabbed her sister's hand, and helped her climb up the plank and onto the ship.

Gus flew up to the crow's nest, opened his beak, made a strange sort of rumbling sound and out shot some flames! The flames lit a wick which lit a fire, which heated the air and filled the deflating hot air balloon until its billowy sides were as wide as their house and as tall as a tree.

The bird looked very proud of himself indeed, until a small puff of wind escaped from his tail feathers. And then he looked rather sheepish.

'Err, cough, bok bok hu hmmmm,' said the bird as he cleared his throat. 'What a strange noise. Must be the frogs.'

'What frogs?' asked an amazed Dot, at which point twenty frogs emerged from the hold of the ship and started untying ropes, deflating landing cushions and releasing the handbrake.

'Hold on tight!' shouted Gus and the girls clung to the side of the ship as it smoothly rose from the roof. Dot looked over the side of the ship at her house from above and said, 'Oh look, that's where all my tennis balls are!'

Higher and higher the ship-cum-balloon flew until the house was just a speck far below them. The heat of the night started to cool the higher they got.

'What kind of a ship is this?' Stella shouted up to the crow's nest as Dot looked over the side and then up to the sky in astonishment.

'This is the *Salvager!*' said Gus most proudly. 'Isn't she tremendous!'

'The *Salvager*,' repeated Dot, scanning the ship in amazement.

15

She certainly was tremendous. The base of the hot air balloon glowed with the light from the fire and the rest of the balloon was a magnificent midnight blue that seemed to have stars in its lining, twinkling as she flew.

'I've never seen a boat like it!' said Dot.

'She's one of a kind,' replied the bird. 'The propellers suck in gravity, spin it around a bit and use it to propel us forward. They whir so fast that the ship disappears from human sight, which is very handy with all the secret missions it does. Yes, we're all very grateful for the *Salvager!*'

Australia was far away now and the girls squeezed one another's hands. 'I'm a bit scared, Stella,' said Dot to her sister, and for once Stella felt unsure too. But then the frogs began to sing while they worked, their cheeks puffing out like balloons, and when they exhaled, a beautiful sound filled the air. First a high-pitched note came from a frog on the ship's mast. It sounded like a child singing in a choir: 'da da daaa da da'. Then a lower note came from another frog, like a rolling of your tongue: 'rratatat aah rratatat aah…' And then an incredible sound emerged from a frog standing close to them as he tied one of the ship's ropes around a post. The noise was so low it was like the rumbling of thunder, the words from a language the girls had never heard before: 'soww doww dootttt, frau dow deeee.'

Stella swallowed and wished the song would never end; nothing had ever made her feel like this before, like she and the frogs and the stars around her were somehow connected. She felt like she was part of something much bigger than just her hometown.

A frog wearing a two cornered hat hopped over to the

girls and handed them a blanket.

'That's Nelson,' said Gus.

'I think he just winked at us,' said Stella, watching his face suspiciously.

'Oh good,' replied Gus. 'That means he likes you.'

Dot shrugged at her big sister. It was too late to be finding singing, winking frogs strange.

It wasn't too long before they were leaving earth's atmosphere when gravity pulled the ship down with a sudden jolt. The girls clung onto the ship but the frogs were prepared and quickly put the ship into second gear. Sparks flew out from its propellers and the ship whizzed upwards even faster than before. Soon planets zipped past – there were orange ones and blue ones, ones with stripes and ones with rings. And the stars! Millions of piercingly bright dots in a sky that changed from black to purple to blue.

'This is incredible,' said Stella under her breath. She wished she had her camera, or her diary and a pen. Her face got very serious trying to remember every detail. Dot, on the other hand, had fallen fast asleep. Stella put her arm around her; as excited as she was, she hoped she wasn't about to get them in trouble.

Chapter Two

'Land ahoy!' shouted one of the frogs after what seemed like no time at all. The children ran to the bow of the ship. The sky became a paler and paler blue as they left space's atmosphere and descended towards the planet called Beatrice. All was green below until Stella and Dot could make out individual trees in a far-reaching forest.

Hu haaaaaaawww, trumpeted a horn from below as children ran out from a house built high up in a tree.

Foooomp, wheezed the rubber cushions as they expanded until firm.

Whizzzz, went the ropes as they slipped through the frogs' suction-y pads.

And *thud*! went the heavy sandbag anchor as it hit the ground below.

The *Salvager* had landed in a giant treehouse. Children waved to the girls from the treehouse deck as tree frogs, birds and squirrels tied the ships' ropes to the branches.

The girls followed Gus down the ship's plank and onto the deck where the children greeted them, cheering.

'Welcome Stella and Dot!' said a beaming little girl at the front. 'I'm Flora, one of the Council members on Beatrice.' Flora didn't look much older than Stella. She had short, spiky hair, freckles on her nose and a pointy little chin that made her look a bit like a pixie. Stella thought Flora really lived up to her name – meaning plants – as the girl had flowers shooting out of her buttonholes and sleeves.

'We're so glad you came!' Flora said. 'Please, make yourselves comfortable.' She offered the girls her hands and led them to an area covered in cushions and rugs. Crystals hung from the branches of the tree and as they caught the sun, rays of light danced around the floor, all the colours of the rainbow. As the breeze blew, wind chimes tinkled magically in the background. It was like a dream but better because they could touch it.

Gus took his seat next to the girls and the children settled in around them. The girls looked at them and realised they were just like them – curious and excited, with wild hair and dirty feet.

'What is this place?' asked Stella, who didn't know where to start.

Flora began to explain, 'Beatrice is a small planet that has given endangered animals from Earth a home for thousands of years. We have baiji white dolphins, pyrenean ibexes, steller's sea cows, great auks…there's a long list. Even some animals that aren't endangered moved here when they'd had enough of all the hardships on Earth.'

'I've never heard of it at school, or at home,' said Stella.

'You wouldn't have,' said Flora. 'Beatrice is completely invisible to Grownups. They don't know it exists. They think most of the animals here are extinct. Beatrice was made to stop that from happening.'

Stella knew something that her mum and dad didn't! She was starting to really like the place.

'Gus has done a few trips to Earth recently and is worried for a great deal of the animals there. We think it's time some more of them were offered a lift here so they can live happily without their homes being destroyed. We wondered if you would help captain the ship and save the animals?'

Stella was amazed. 'I'd love to…but we have to go to school.'

'Maybe she doesn't care about animals after all,' said a boy who had been staring rudely at both the girls. His long dark hair blew across his face and he pushed it away angrily. His clothes were made from fur and he was covered in mud, his shins speckled with bruises.

'I do care about animals,' said Stella, staring straight back at the boy. 'I've only ever wanted to be a vet and help animals. I happen to like animals a lot more than I like people.' And she arched her eyebrow at him in a way that she hoped said, "especially you".

'I wouldn't want Mum and Dad to worry,' said Dot.

'They wouldn't. They'd never know you were gone,' said Flora, her kind face was reassuring. 'Gus would come and get you for missions and have you back before they even noticed. The ship's clever like that.'

'But if we told them I'm sure they'd underst—'

'No!' interrupted the boy, making Dot jump.

'Don't shout at my sister!' shouted Stella. It was getting rather loud.

Gus flapped up to her side. 'He doesn't mean any harm. I'm sorry he startled you both. This is Fauna, he's very protective of Beatrice.' Gus looked at the boy. 'Fauna, you should apologise.'

'Sorry,' Fauna mumbled.

Just like Flora, who clearly loved plants, Stella thought Fauna also lived up to his name which meant animals. He looked predatory, like he would be at home living with a pack of wolves.

Gus continued. 'We just have a rule that Grownups don't know about us. Sometimes, the more they know the more harm they do. We have to make sure we keep Planet Beatrice safe. Life is simple here – there are no buildings or machines – and that's how it must stay.'

'The future is more important to us than Grownups. We know what really matters. Sometimes Grownups forget,' added Flora.

'Mum and Dad are kind people, though,' Dot continued quietly. 'They're vets too. They wouldn't hurt anyone.'

'I don't doubt that little miss,' said Gus gently, 'but that is the rule, I'm afraid. We will understand if you don't feel it is for you.'

Stella looked at her sister. 'Can we have a minute?' she asked Flora.

'Of course,' replied the girl. 'Please take your time. We're so grateful that you came.'

The Council left, leaving the girls to talk. They walked over to the edge of the deck and leant on the banister, looking out at the trees. It was a hot day and the air was heavy and sticky. Birds flew at their eye level and monkeys swung from the limbs of the trees. They had never seen so much wildlife. Now the bush where they lived seemed quite quiet.

'I don't like that boy,' said Stella.

'No,' replied her sister, 'but you don't like loads of boys at school and it doesn't stop you from going.'

'That's true,' said Stella. 'It would be so dangerous.'

'But exciting…' said Dot.

21

'You'll get tired…'

'I won't complain.'

'You'll forget and tell Mum and Dad.'

'I won't, I promise. I like it here. I want to help them.'

'Me too,' replied Stella.

'And now I know the adventures we could be having, I think I'd be sad not having them.'

And Stella realised that that would be unbearable. 'Okay,' she said, 'let's try it. But if I decide that we should go home, we will. Deal?'

'Deal!' Dot said with delight and shouted, 'Woohoooo!' very loudly.

The Council all came running at the noise.

'Have you decided?' asked Flora.

'Yes,' said Stella. 'We accept your offer. We'd love to help.'

The children jumped up and cheered. The birds and the frogs sang, the squirrels danced and Gus let out an excited accidental puff of wind from his tail. He pointed to the horizon and said, 'Oh! Look at that interesting cloud…'

Flora held the girls' hands. 'This is such wonderful news. So many animals will be grateful, just as we are. It's a really important job, and one you won't be able to do unless you can talk to the animals and understand them. Just as you do with Gus.'

'That was easy, we understood him straight away,' said an overly confident Stella. 'Maybe we can understand all the animals here now.'

'Try it,' said Fauna, smirking to himself.

A squirrel scurried past and Stella cleared her throat. 'Hu hummm, excuse me!' The squirrel continued on his way. 'Um, excuse me!' Stella tried again a little louder and the squirrel turned around. 'My name's Stella, what's yours?' The squirrel squeaked and Stella turned red.

'I have to give you the power to talk with other animals, girls,' said Gus. 'Are you sure you're ready?'

'Yes!' said the girls together. Stella wondered what her pet rabbit would say.

'Okay then,' said the bird. 'You'd better sit down.' The girls sat on the floor and held hands.

Gus began to dance. His feet jigged up and down as if he was standing on hot coals and he flapped his wings with increasing urgency. Soon he started to sing, 'Haarrrrr bok bok haarrrr bok bok,' faster and faster, and louder and louder until his wings were a blur and dust swirled around him and the girls. 'HAARRRRR BOK BOK HAARRRRRRR!'

Suddenly he stopped and collapsed on the floor. He looked up and placed his wings on the girls' shoulders. He opened his beak and an orange mist surrounded the three of them. 'I give you this power to talk to the animal kingdom. Use it for good, or it will go.'

'We will,' said Stella.

'We promise,' said Dot.

The mist settled and all was calm. The squirrel came towards the girls.

'My name's James,' he said. 'Nice to meet you.'

Dot was just opening her mouth to respond when she was interrupted by the blare of a trumpet. *Hu haaaaaaawwwww!* it went.

'What's that?' Dot asked.

'That sound announces the beginning of a celebratory

feast!' declared James.

'You're joining the Council of Planet Beatrice,' grinned Gus.

The treehouse erupted into a party. A band of toucans picked up some instruments and started playing jazz music while a Bengal tiger slowly made her way to the stage. Lemurs breakdanced and chimpanzees tangoed. The tiger picked up a microphone and purred into it and all on the deck went wild! Stella's mouth was open wide with astonishment. Her legs couldn't help but dance. A young boy yanked on her pyjamas pulling her face down level to his. He laughed, stuck his finger in a pot of purple goo and wiped stripes of it on her nose and cheeks. She was deciding whether or not to tell him off when she saw Dot out of the corner of her eye, laughing with delight, her face covered in goo. Stella smiled at the little boy and he toddled off to paint the rest of the Council tribe.

Brummm brr-brr-brummmm went the beat of the drums as some monkeys hit them rhythmically with their hands and feet. Animals were hurrying in and out of a door in the trunk of the treehouse. Two birds flew past Stella towards it and she caught a snippet of their conversation:

'...starving, hope they've got those potato waffles again....'

'Stop it, my beak's watering just thinking about it....'

Stella went to have a look. She peered through the entrance and saw a huge kitchen. The tree was hollow on the inside! Children were stirring massive pots of bubbling soup, frogs were stoking a fire, and a sloth was shelling some peas. Stella stared at him as he tried to open the pea shells with his long fingernails.

'I know,' he said through a wide yawn. 'It's a terrible job, I don't know whyyyyy they give it to me.' Peas flew everywhere; the sloth laid his head on the kitchen table and went to sleep.

Hundreds of little candles sat in carved out nooks in the tree, making everything glow warmly. The smell of food was unbelievably delicious and the kitchen was packed. Stella moved around the room, trying not to get in anyone's way.

'Oh, I'm sorry, excuse me,' she said as she backed into something and then gulped when she realized it was a jaguar. His remarkable orange and black fur rippled as he moved and his piercing green eyes locked on her grey ones. Her heart skipped a beat, she started to back away…

'No problem, Stella,' said the jaguar and continued patting dough with his paw. He used one of his claws to cut the dough into balls. Stella hadn't breathed for a while. 'Bread rolls,' he said.

'Of course,' she replied, unsure of the right thing to say to a baking jaguar.

A stack of bowls greeted her. 'Hi, Stella, lovely of you to join us!' Stella looked behind the bowls and found a little girl carrying them.

'Can I help?' she asked.

'Oh, yes please!' The girl handed Stella the stack. 'Can you take these out to the deck?'

'No problem!' Stella headed to the door.

She'd almost made it outside when something pushed past her and stuck its leg out in front of her foot. She fought to keep her balance but couldn't and landed on her knees, all the bowls clattering to the floor. The little girl ran over to help her. 'I'm so sorry,' she said. 'I gave you too many.'

'It wasn't that,' said Stella, 'something tripped me up.'
She looked around the room. All the animals were
continuing with their work. It was a hive of activity, the
entire room filled with movement.

'There's always someone in your way in the kitchen,'
explained the girl. 'Everyone wants to be in here, especially
in winter.' But Stella was only half listening. She'd spotted
Fauna with a boy and a girl; they were looking at her and
smiling nastily from the across the room. Had they tripped
her over?

Stella picked herself up and decided she'd ignore them
for now. She had no proof it was Fauna that had tripped her
up, just a feeling that he was to blame.

She helped the girl pick up the bowls and they carried
them outside. 'I'm Bramble,' said the girl, 'it's so good to
meet you. We've been waiting ages for Gus and the Council
to find the right child to help the animals, and now they've
found two!'

'Ohhhh, Dot! I've forgotten all about my sister. Do you
know where she is?' Stella couldn't believe she hadn't kept
an eye on her. She looked around frantically.

'Up there,' said Bramble and pointed to a swing above
them. It was tied high up in the tree so that it swung the
whole length of the deck. On the swing next to Dot sat Gus,
his tail feathers blowing in the breeze as they swung. Dot
was always smiling but Stella didn't think she'd ever seen
her smile this wide before.

Children and frogs poured out of the kitchen carrying
dish after dish of delicious treats. Baked potatoes and
sweetcorn, bowls of peanut butter and stacks of toast, bright

coloured vegetables and sticky honey-covered bananas. The frogs had arranged the cushions in a large circle and all the children hurried to a long table to scoop the food into their bowls and find a place to sit. Stella found her sister in the throng and gave her a hug. As much as she sometimes found her younger sister annoying, she was really glad she was here.

The girls looked around for somewhere to sit and saw Flora waving to them to join. The girls took their seats opposite Flora and a boy who introduced himself as River. 'It's good to finally meet you,' he said. 'So, what do you think so far?'

'Ummm, it's quite a lot to take in,' said Stella.

'Well, I think it's the best place in the whole world,' said Dot. 'Wait, we're not in the world, are we? I think it's the best place in all the worlds.'

'How did you find us?' asked Stella. 'I mean, why us?'

'Your magazine, "The Planet: How to Stop Ruining It",' said Flora. 'The title really caught our attention.' Stella had started a magazine out of recycled paper at school. Strangely enough it wasn't particularly popular but that hadn't put her off.

'We were looking for someone who felt strongly about animals and the environment,' said River.

'Why not one of the Council?'

'It takes all of us to look after Planet Beatrice, and we needed someone who knows Earth.'

'What about me?' asked Dot. 'How can I help? I hope I don't slow you down,' she said to Stella, her eyes welling up.

'You won't,' said Stella. 'I'm sorry if it sometimes feels

27

like that. I'm really glad you're here.'

'Us too,' said Flora. 'When we heard Stella had a sister with such a big heart, we were absolutely convinced you two were just what we needed.'

Dot beamed. 'Thank you!' she squealed and launched herself over her bowl to hug everyone. Stella could feel her dinner spill into her lap and she brushed it off before Dot could see.

When everyone had finished eating, Flora and Dot tidied the table and Stella and River took the bowls into the kitchen to wash up. River scrubbed the bowls in soapy water and handed them to Stella to rinse. She looked at him as he washed. He had very short blond hair that looked like it had been shaved and deep-set eyes that made it hard to read his expression. But standing so close to him Stella could see his eyes were bright blue, as if a light shone behind them. He made her feel nervous and she wasn't sure why. She wasn't normally shy around boys.

'So, what's Australia like?' he asked.

'It's cool, y'know?' That was a strange thing for her to say, she thought. He didn't know at all, that's why he was asking. 'I mean, it's pretty boring really.' Aah! What was she doing? It's not boring at all! She felt herself starting to go red. 'It's not boring. Actually, it's fantastic. You should come visit some time!'

She was going to have to stop talking soon if her mouth insisted on saying silly things.

River smiled. 'Maybe. I kind of like it here though.' Stella turned a deeper shade of red.

For some reason, this boy turned her into an idiot. *Stop right now*, she thought to herself. *Be normal.*

28

'What do you do on Beatrice? And why's it called Beatrice anyway?' she asked.

'We call it, Bea. It's named after a girl, Beatrice.' River looked away. Stella thought he looked sad all of a sudden. She wondered who this girl Beatrice was and was just about to ask when River turned back to look at her, his eyes shining brighter than ever.

'I'm a forager: I find food for us in the forest. We're vegetarian here so finding and growing enough food is important. There's a gardening team that grows fruit and vegetables and I find ingredients that grow in the wild. Mushrooms, nuts, berries, plants…it's incredible how much is out there.'

'And you can tell what's poisonous?' She realized she'd have to wait to find out more about Beatrice.

'Yes, some plants are poisonous. I'm pretty good at telling them apart. I can teach you some time if you'd like?'

'That would be good.' A new sensation was stirring in Stella's tummy at the thought of spending more time with River; it was a mixture of very excited and a bit like she might throw up.

They finished washing their bowls and walked outside. Dot and Gus came towards them.

'Stella, my dear, I think it's time we got you girls home.'

Now that Gus had said it, Stella realised just how tired she was. 'Perhaps. But we'll come back?'

Gus nodded. 'Oh yes, we do hope so, we have to prepare you for your first mission.'

Stella had a rush of nerves, there was a lot she had to learn and she didn't want to fail.

Gus seemed to read her mind. 'You have the power to speak to and understand all the animals now. When you are ready for the job, you must listen to their stories and tell them about us. Tell them there's hope.'

'We will,' said Stella, determined to do everything she could to help.

'We have a game of Leap Frog coming up too, that'll be good training,' River said. 'You've got to come back for that!'

'Can't wait,' Stella replied feeling determined.

'Right,' said Gus, 'let's get these girls home.'

'See you later, Stella,' said River.

'Bye, River.'

'What's wrong with you?' asked Dot. 'Why is your face all stupid and happy?'

'Shut up,' said Stella still smiling.

The girls boarded the ship and the frogs released the ropes, allowing the *Salvager* to rise gently from the deck of the treehouse, its balloon now emerald green.

'Goodbye,' came shouts from the deck. 'See you sooooonnn!'

The girls waved goodbye to the extraordinary children and animals below. The ship's pace increased and it whizzed up into space. The girls slumped against the wall and Gus covered them in blankets. Incapable of keeping their eyes open they drifted off to sleep only to be woken moments later by Gus' feathery touch.

'We're home, girls.'

As the rubber cushions touched down on the roof of the girls' house, Gus hugged them both with his soft warm wings.

'Now you two get a proper sleep, and remember, not a word to anyone. I shall be back in a week. I think you'll really like a game of Leap Frog.'

'Goodnight, Gus,' said Dot, yawning.

'Goodnight, Gus,' said Stella.

The girls kissed him goodbye and climbed down the trellis into their room. They had so much to talk about, but it would have to wait. Stella climbed into her bed and looked at the clock, it was 11.37p.m. Had they really just been gone minutes? She tried to understand but couldn't work anything more out for the day. She fell fast asleep.

Chapter Three

'Girls! Wake up, you'll be late for school!'

Stella heard her mother walking down the hallway, she opened her eyes. Please tell me it wasn't a dream, she thought to herself.

'Are you both all right? I've never known you to sleep in before.'

'Ughhh.' Dot groaned from her bed.

Stella looked at Dot and could just see under Dot's mop of hair her face was smeared in purple goo. Stella touched her own face and darted under the covers. 'We're fine, Mum,' said Stella, trying to keep her voice normal. 'We'll be dressed soon.'

'Good,' said their mother turning back towards the kitchen. 'Please don't turn into teenagers just yet.'

Stella rushed over to Dot's bed and pulled back the covers. 'Dot, wake up!'

'What is it, I'm so sleeepy...' Suddenly, she shot out of bed. 'Wait, what happened? Is Gus back? Was it real?' Dot saw her sister's purple face.

'It was real,' said Stella.

'Oh my goodness, Stella! I can't believe it really happened and it was so amazing! The *Salvager* and Planet Bea and that rude boy, but everyone else was soooo cool and, and, the treehouse and space!'

'I know, I know, but we've got to be normal and go and

eat breakfast and just CALM DOWN.'

'Okay, okay, I can do this. What do I do?'

'Go and wash your face, and legs and everything; in fact, have a shower. I'll get your backpack ready.'

The girls got ready for school and walked into the kitchen where their father was reading some papers and their mother was eyeing them suspiciously. 'Toast or a muesli bar?' she asked them.

Dot stood frozen to the spot staring at her sister.

'Toast,' said Stella.

'Toast,' repeated Dot, grinning maniacally.

'Aren't you forgetting something?' said their mother and both girls froze. *'What did I forget?'* thought Stella. She touched her face.

'Please?' said their mother.

'Please what?' asked Stella.

'Toast please. Please can I have some toast. What is wrong with you two today?' She came over and felt their foreheads. Stella thought Dot was about to explode. 'You feel fine but maybe you shouldn't go to school.'

'No, we're good, honestly.' The thought of being home with her mother all day and acting normal was too much for Stella.

'Right. Well take your toast and off you go or you'll miss the bus.' She turned to the girls' father. 'Your daughters are acting very strange, Greg. I think they take after your side of the family.'

Stella and Dot grabbed the toast and ran out of the front door, down the lane and made it to the bus stop just as the school bus was pulling in. Stella saw her best friend Zara wave to her from the back seat, signalling that she'd saved her a spot. But instead of joining her she bundled Dot into a two-seater at the front.

'What are you doing?' asked Dot.

'I just want to make sure we don't say anything we shouldn't.'

'I won't! I promised, didn't I?' Dot lowered her voice to a loud whisper. 'But wasn't it incredible? What was your favourite bit? I think mine was space. No, the feast. Oooh ooh no, maybe it's talking to the animals...'

'Shhh...' Stella tried to stop her in time, but it was too late.

'You're talking to animals now are you, Dot?' The mean girl from Dot's year, Alicia, was leaning in from the seat behind them. 'I always thought you were nuts.'

Stella and Dot turned around and saw a group of girls on the seats behind them laughing.

'Dotty's a bit potty. Potty dotty,' Alicia sang, and the girls joined in.

'Shut up!' said Dot, tears in her eyes.

'Stop it, Alicia,' said Stella. 'Dot said she talked to the animals at Mum and Dad's vet, she didn't say they talked back. Maybe you're the one that's a bit crazy.'

The girls stopped singing and one of them laughed, Alicia shot her a livid look.

'Wait until I tell my big sister, Stella Peters. She'll make mincemeat out of you.'

'Well, she'd have to turn up to school to do that, which is unlikely given she's always suspended, so I think I'll be all right.'

Stella and Dot turned around in their seats and Stella squeezed her sister's hand on her lap. As the bus pulled into school and everyone piled out through the gates, Stella pulled Dot aside.

'I'll be in the library at lunch break if you need me, okay?'

Dot nodded, her eyes still red.

'If Alicia's mean to you just ignore her. Or better still just smile, that'll really confuse the dummy.' Stella smiled at her sister and Dot smiled back weakly. She watched Dot walk off into the netball court where all the students were running around chasing each other and looking at their phones. Stella wished they were back on Bea.

'Hey Zara!' she called out after her best friend.

'Why didn't you come and sit with me?'

'Sorry, just had to chat to Dot.'

'Well, you need to chat to me too, I've got something so exciting to tell you!' Stella wondered what it could be: a talking bird that breathed fire, a jaguar making bread rolls...

'I got a new bike yesterday and the helmet's a shark!'

Stella looked unimpressed.

'What? It's got fins and everything.' Stella took a big breath; this was going to be a long day.

That night the girls climbed into bed, exhausted at having had to keep such incredible secrets.

'I know why it's called Planet Beatrice,' Stella said quietly to her sister.

'Why?'

'It was named after a girl called Beatrice.'

'Who told you that?'

'River.'

'Ooohhh, Riivvveerrr,' Dot sang.

'You're so immature, Dot.'

'Good, isn't it.' Dot laughed.

'Well anyway, there's something really interesting about it, about Beatrice. I'm going to find out more.'

'Cool,' said Dot. 'I'm going to go to sleep.'

'Night, Dot. Sweet dreams.'

'Night, Stella. You too.'

Chapter Four

A few nights later the girls woke to the sound of another thud on the roof.

The girls sat straight up in bed. 'He's back!' they both said, buzzing with excitement. They climbed out of the window, onto the trellis and up onto the roof. There was the *Salvager*, its balloon twinkling like diamonds. The frogs sat along the wall of the ship and in the middle, stood Gus.

'Hello friends,' he said and they ran up the plank to hug him. 'You ready for Leap Frog?'

'Absolutely,' said Stella, smiling.

'I was born ready!' shouted Dot as she jumped from the top of the plank and landed on the floor of the ship with a crash.

Stella shook her head. 'Let's get going.'

The *Salvager* took off and zipped into space with a flash. The frogs started to sing and the girls' faces ached with such huge grins – they were going back to Planet Bea!

As the planets hurtled past Stella kept an eye out for the white and brown swirls of Pluto and when she saw it, she knew they were near Planet Bea. She squinted her eyes until, there! She saw the tiny planet, blues and greens and browns and growing bigger by the second. 'We're here,' she said under her breath. It already felt like a second home.

Down and down the *Salvager* flew, whooshing towards the green of the rainforest and finally slowing as it neared the huge treehouse. All the children and animals rushed out onto the deck and waved like mad – Stella and Dot were back!

The frogs threw out the plank and the girls stepped onto the deck to be greeted by hundreds of welcoming hands, paws and wings. Flora, River and Bramble led the girls to the cushions and gave them lemonade with mint and buttery biscuits.

'How was home?' asked Flora.

'Same old,' said Stella. 'Pretty boring after seeing this place.'

'I didn't tell anyone anything about it, I did really well!' said Dot.

'Well done, Dot.' Flora smiled.

Stella forced herself to look at River confidently.

'It's nice to see you again,' he said.

'You too,' smiled Stella, squeezing her sister's hand so she wouldn't say anything embarrassing.

'Hey, Gus!' called Fauna. Stella hadn't missed him. She recognised the children standing next to him as the same ones from the kitchen when she'd been tripped over.

'So, are they going to play Leap Frog or not?' he said tauntingly. There was a murmur of excitement from the crowd.

'It's up to them, Fauna. They might want to take their time.'

'Awww, are they scared?' Fauna pretended to cry and his two friends laughed.

Stella had never cared about sports before but all of a sudden she cared very much. 'We used to do Leap Frog all the time at school. When we were like, babies.'

'Maybe it's for babies on Earth,' replied Fauna, 'but not on Bea.'

'Okay sure, I'll play,' she retorted, trying not to listen to the bit of her that thought this might be a bad idea.

'I want to play too!' shouted Dot who despite being quite clumsy was unbelievably competitive and fearless. This made her exhilarating to watch, except if you were her parents, and then it was just plain terrifying.

'All right then,' said Gus. 'It will help you both feel prepared for your first mission to save animals from earth if you learn how to work with them, trust them and move like them. But remember, Leap Frog is just a game, it's the taking part that matters, not the winning.' Stella, Dot and Fauna agreed, none of them really agreeing at all.

'Right, these are the rules,' said Flora. 'There are two teams of four players. Each player is at a different post in the forest. The first player has to get to the second player and when he or she reaches them, then the second player can go to the third and then the third to the fourth. Then the fourth has to get to the final post and the first team to get there, wins.'

'Why is it called Leap Frog?' asked Stella

'Because the tricky part is you're not allowed to touch the ground.'

'So how do you get anywhere if you can't walk or run?'

'Well, you have to be like a tree frog: climb and leap!'

'Right. The thing is, frogs have sticky pads on their hands and feet. I'm not sure about children on Bea but children on Earth don't.'

'We don't either,' said Flora, 'but we do have these.' A frog wearing a hat wheeled a chest towards them.

39

'Is that Nelson?' Dot asked her sister.

''ello, ladies,' said Nelson, and gave them another wink.

Talking to animals was starting to feel less strange. 'Hi Nelson.'

'This is one of Gus' excellent inventions.' Flora rummaged in the chest and turned around wearing giant orange rubbery gloves with big, sticky pads on the palms.

'Ugh are we washing up again?' groaned Dot and Flora laughed.

'They're not for washing up, they're for sticking to vines and trees. You just wait. It is so. Much. Fun.' She took her gloves off and helped Dot put on her own pair. Dot waved her hands in the air just as a parrot was flying past. The parrot immediately stuck to her glove and squawked, 'Oi!'

'Oh, I'm so sorry,' said Dot and tried to unstick him with her other glove. Now the parrot was stuck in two sticky hands and had had quite enough.

'Please let go of me!' the parrot wriggled helplessly, green and red feathers floating to the floor.

'Here,' said Stella, 'let me help.' She peeled back her sister's gloved fingers and the parrot flew up in the air.

'Honestly,' he said, flying off, leaving behind a brown and white dollop that dropped onto the ground between the sisters.

'Good luck?' joked Stella, hoping to reassure them both.

'You don't have to play if you don't want to,' said Fauna.

'We want to,' said the girls in unison.

'Perfect,' said Flora. 'I'll be on your team and who else…Bramble, do you want to join us?'

'Definitely,' said Bramble with a smile.

'I'll captain the other team,' said Fauna. 'I choose Skyla, Lark…' Fauna's mean-looking friends stepped forward, 'and River.' Stella was startled at the sound of River's name – were he and Fauna friends? She couldn't help but feel confused and a little hurt.

'What about the animals?' asked Dot. 'Do they play?'

'They move the posts,' replied Flora. 'It's more fun when you don't know the way.'

The little boy who had painted goo on their faces for the feast made his way over to the girls carrying two big tubs. 'Which team do you want to be, blue or orange?' he asked Dot.

'Orange please.' She knelt down and the little boy rubbed orange goo all over her face. 'What's in it?'

'Apricot, melon and slime.'

'Great!' said Dot.

The boy covered the rest of the orange team's faces and then moved on to Fauna and the blue team. When he was finished Stella felt a little uneasy; their blue faces looked quite frightening. River was looking at her but she turned away. Maybe she'd imagined that he liked her. Maybe he and Fauna were laughing at her.

She decided she was going to win this game.

'Come on,' said Flora, 'let me show you how to use these gloves.' They walked over to the edge of the deck and opened a gate that led onto a launching pad. Several vines were tied to a post and Flora untied them and handed them to the girls. 'It's really very easy. You just hold on and push off. Watch.'

Flora held onto a vine and leapt off the launching pad. The sight of her flying through the forest was incredible and the girls couldn't wait to have a go. She swung back to the launching pad and said, 'Who's next?'

'Me, me, me,' shouted Dot. But Stella had other ideas.

'Hold on, Dot, I'd better go first.' Ordinarily she wouldn't dream of doing something so reckless, but she wasn't going to let that boy beat her.

'Boring,' said Dot, folding her arms and getting her hands stuck to her pyjamas.

With her sister tied up, Stella took her vine and jumped off the pad. She hardly had to grip at all, the gloves stuck so tight to the vine. Her legs flew out behind her as she whizzed through the air. 'This is amaaaaaazzziiiiinnnngggg,' she sang. She had studied birds all her life and she'd always wondered what it would be like to fly, and this was as close as she was likely to get. She listened to the sounds of a million creatures talking to each other. She had never seen so many shades of green or a forest so thick!

The vine eased to a halt before it began swinging back towards the treehouse. It gathered speed and she could see her sister, Flora and Bramble getting bigger and bigger. But then the vine started to slow and she wasn't sure she'd reach them!

Flora was hanging on to the post of the treehouse with one of her gloved hands and with the other leant out and grabbed Stella's hand just as her toes touched the pad. 'I've got you. Just concentrate on your hands and think "let go",' said Flora. Stella looked down at the vast canopy of leaves below her. She couldn't even see the ground they were so high up. 'It's all right,' said Flora and Stella trusted her. She held on to Flora and let go of the vine as Flora pulled her back onto the pad.

'What happens if you can't make it back to the treehouse? What happens if you're just left swinging from a vine forever?' Stella demanded. She was angry with herself for not thinking about that before she made the leap.

'There are nets all around the treehouse, and the frogs tie nets between the posts when they set up a game of Leap Frog. They'll catch you if you fall.'

'If or when?' asked Stella.

'Probably when.' Flora smiled. 'To be good at Leap Frog sometimes you have to leap.'

Stella wasn't convinced, but before she could stop her Dot had taken her vine and was soaring away from the treehouse.

'Be careful!' Stella shouted after her.

'Wooohooooo!' screamed Dot. Stella watched as her sister swung through the forest. Her long arms and legs were like ropes themselves and the higher and the faster she went the louder her screams of excitement became. Stella gasped as Dot let go of the vine and soared through the air, her hands reaching out to grasp the branch of a tree. She pulled herself up, sat on the branch and looked around.

'What are you doing!' yelled Stella, cupping her hands to her mouth.

'Talking to an orangutan!' came a faint reply.

Stella watched as Dot swung to another tree, hooked her legs over the branch and fell backwards so she was dangling upside down. 'That's it, come back right now!'

43

Stella looked at Flora. 'I should have tied her to the post.'

'She's coming back!' said Bramble. Leaves rustled and a wind started to blow.

'There she is!' said Flora as Dot came into view, one arm holding a vine and the other waving madly at them. She jumped and landed on the launchpad.

'That was so cool!' she said.

'Oh yeah, fantastic.' Stella exhaled. She was hugely relieved, quite proud and a little bit jealous.

'I saw the nets, Stella!'

'Well, that's something,' said Stella, knowing that she should probably stop all of this right now. But she couldn't quite bring herself to do so.

'The posts are nearly in position,' reported Nelson. 'Ten more minutes until leap off!'

'Time to go to the stadium,' said Flora.

'Stadium?' said Dot.

'Yes,' said Flora proudly. 'It's on the other side of the tree. Let's go!'

The girls left the deck and started the journey to the stadium. They climbed some stairs that led up onto a balcony wrapped around the huge treehouse. It would take ten minutes just to get to the other side. Children and animals hung out of windows in the trunk of the tree, wishing them good luck.

'Go, Stella!'

'Good luck, Dot!'

'Go, team orange!'

Soon they started to hear the noise of the crowd. Hundreds of children, birds and animals packed seats that overlooked the forest. A giant launching pad hung out over

44

the side of the tree, blue and orange banners streaming from the posts. The girls were practically hopping with excitement. But then they saw Fauna and the blue team and their hearts sank. They had never played before, how could they possibly beat them?

Gus shuffled towards them.

'Boy am I glad to see you!' said Stella.

'There's nothing to fear, dear girl. These trees are packed with birds and animals that are your friends.'

And one boy who definitely isn't, she thought.

A small animal that looked like a possum with wings glided through the air towards them.

'You have flying possums here!' said Dot. 'Awesome!'

'That's a sugar glider,' said Stella, as the sugar glider landed gently on her shoulder.

'Salam!' he declared.

'That means peace,' Stella added to Dot.

'That's right, clever of you to know. My name's Batara.' He extended a tiny hand and the girls shook it. In his other hand he had a fistful of sticks.

'I'm the stick master,' Batara said, puffing out his chest with pride. 'Please pick a stick to find out which post you are.'

The four girls drew sticks. 'The shortest one's first post,' said Batara.

'That's me,' said Bramble. Dot was second, Flora third and Stella fourth. The frogs brought the girls their gloves and they put them on.

'I'll stay here as I'm first post,' explained Bramble. 'When the horn signals the start of the game I'll look for an orange light in a tree, that's where second post will be. The blue team will look for blue lights. But the finals post is lit by a red light. That's what you'll be looking for, Stella.'

Suddenly three eagles flew from the forest and landed on the deck.

'Now what happens?' asked Stella. The eagles weren't making her feel any less nervous.

'Now we carry you to your posts,' replied the harpy eagle. The eagles each picked up a rope that was attached to a sling.

'Jump on,' said the golden eagle. Stella looked at him suspiciously.

'It's okay,' added the African crowned eagle, 'we won't bite.'

'Or drop you,' said the golden eagle, laughing.

'Or rip you to shreds,' cackled the harpy. They were all finding it very funny now.

'Now,' said Flora, 'no teasing. You can take me first, Aerie,' Flora said to the eagles.

'It is quite eerie isn't it,' said Dot.

'No, *Aerie*. It's the name for a group of eagles. They're big softies really, I promise.'

The girls watched as three more eagles landed next to the blue team. Somehow their eagles didn't look like they made many jokes. Stella dared herself to look at Fauna and River; they were both staring at her. She stared back for a second, not wanting to seem afraid, then looked away just as River started to…smile? She wasn't sure but she wasn't going to look back. She didn't know what anyone on that team was up to, she just had to focus on herself and the orange team.

Flora climbed into the sling and the eagles took off, one

in front, one in the middle and one behind, their massive wing spans almost bigger than Stella and Dot put together.

'See you soon girls. Just relax, it'll be fun!' Off the eagles flew into the trees, the girls watching as their new friend got smaller and smaller, Flora giving one last wave before she disappeared from sight. Stella wished she wasn't new to this game and looked as confident as Flora did.

After a little while a high-pitched bell rang.

'She's made it,' said Gus. Then they heard a deep, clanging bell. 'That's the blue team, they've made it to their post.'

The eagles returned and dropped the sling, their claws landing on the deck with a heavy scratch. They folded their gigantic wings back in and turned to look at Dot.

'Your turn Dot. Ring the bell when you get there,' said Gus.

'You don't have to do this, Dot,' said Stella.

'It's all right. I'm good at this, remember?'

The sisters hugged and Dot climbed into the sling.

'Let's go!' she shouted, and the eagles swooped into the forest. Stella stared at them until she couldn't see them anymore. She thought about Dot swinging so happily from the trees earlier and tried to convince herself she'd be okay. She closed her eyes and wished her sister would be safe. An image of her mum popped into her head and she tried to shake it away. 'I'll look after her better, I promise,' she said to her mum quietly.

It felt like forever before Stella heard another tinkly bell ring. It sounded far away.

'She's at the second post,' said Gus. 'Your turn, dear girl.'

47

The eagles returned and lowered the sling; the crowd went wild. Stella turned around to look at the auditorium. She squinted into the sun and saw a huge throng of creatures jumping and shouting encouragement and a deafening din of hoots and yelps. But in the sea of orange, she could also make out some blue faces which sent shivers down her spine.

She took a big breath. 'Here goes nothing!' she said and lay down on the sling and held onto the ropes as the eagles launched off the pad. Her stomach flipped at the sudden jolt, her hands gripping the ropes as tightly as she could. She looked up at the eagles' bellies. Their wings looked incredibly powerful from up close and their claws incredibly sharp. She felt the wind on her face as they picked up speed. She looked down, trying to catch a glimpse of a net, but couldn't see anything other than green. The eagles turned from left to right to dodge the trees, Stella swinging as they moved.

She saw movement up ahead and as she got closer, she realised it was Dot waving her arms. She was sitting on a branch next to an orange light and a bell, looking perfectly at home. They flew past Dot and Stella yelled out, 'Be careful!'

'Good luck, Stella!' her sister called out, already far behind her. The eagles dipped down now. The third post was lower: Dot would have to climb or leap down to reach Flora, who waved to her as she passed.

Now the eagles veered to the right and up again higher into the trees. There was an orange light ahead and the eagles headed towards it. They landed on a branch and Stella climbed shakily out into the limbs of a tree. She spotted a bell hanging next to the light.

'Ring the bell so they know you're here,' said the harpy. 'When they hear yours and the blue team's bell at the treehouse they'll signal the horn to start the game. You can be looking for the red light while you wait for Flora. That's the final post.'

'Good luck,' said the golden eagle. 'I hope you win.' And with that they flew up higher and higher until they reached the top of the trees and were off into the clear blue skies. Stella rang her bell, its sweet noise cutting through the sounds of the forest.

She looked around. A sugar glider was sitting right behind her, making her jump. 'Don't fall yet!' he giggled and jumped off his branch, gliding beautifully through the air. Her heart was racing with nerves and the thrill of everything that was happening. She was sitting high up in a tree in a tropical rain forest, surrounded by animals, and she'd just been carried here by eagles! No one would believe her at school even if she was allowed to tell them.

Suddenly a low, ominous bell rang, making her shudder. It sounded like it was close – Fauna was nearby. She searched the trees for him.

Ha hauwwwww. She heard the horn back at the treehouse. The game had started.

Stella imagined Bramble taking her vine and throwing herself out into the forest. She really liked Bramble and Flora and didn't want to let them down. She felt this game was a test to see how well she could do, whether she really was the best person for the job. She took a deep breath and closed her eyes, willing herself to focus on her courage. The sound of the orange team's second post bell chimed faintly in the distance. Dot would be playing now. Stella opened her eyes and felt calm, she imagined she was an eagle. She would not be scared. A blue team's bell: they were hot on Dot's heels. 'Go Dot,' she said under her breath, squeezing her fingers into her palms.

Stella kept looking through the forest, taking in every detail. It smelled earthy like her dad's greenhouse, and it was humid and moist. Beads of sweat gathered on her forehead. She took her gloves off and rolled the sleeves of her pyjamas up. She felt that the forest had an energy, like it was vibrating. A colony of ants marched around her on the branch of a tree, they were carrying at least ten times their bodyweight. They were so tiny but so strong. 'Go you,' she said to them and put her gloves back on.

Another orange team bell: Dot had made it to the third post. Stella concentrated on the direction the noise came from, trying to imagine Flora's route. She felt instinctively that she knew where Flora would emerge from and just like that, Flora burst through the trees.

'Over here, Flora!' Stella waved her arms and caught Flora as she landed in the tree. Flora rang the bell and then both girls froze as they heard the blue team's fourth post bell. Fauna would be searching for the red light right now too.

'Go Stella, find the red light!'

Stella grabbed a vine and swung out into the trees, she had to find the red light before Fauna. Sun beams pierced through the green leaves from the sky above and Stella thought she saw bright red lights everywhere, but it was just fruit hanging from the trees.

She kept swinging and swinging, desperately searching

left and right. She wasn't looking where she was going and crashed through some tangled branches, twigs scratching her arms. She swung into a clearing and it gave her a chance to see properly. A parrot flew past her and her eyes followed its path. Wait! What was that? High up above in the forest to the left, the red light! How could she get there? She grabbed another vine so that she had one in each hand and started to swing one way and then another to build momentum. She let go of one vine and grabbed another, pulling herself towards the final post. She was going to make it; she was nearly there!

Then suddenly a force crashed into her and she was spinning out of control. She held on for dear life as she spun around and around.

The vine creaked from above and then *snap*! It broke and she was hurtling rapidly to the ground. She desperately tried to grab onto anything that she passed but only managed to get a handful of leaves before hitting the net below, knocking some of the air out of her lungs. She bounced up and down a few times before she came to a halt, lying on her back and looking up at the trees. She heard the fourth post bell ring and tears welled in her eyes.

Plop! Something landed on the net next to her.

'Nelson?'

'Hello, sweetheart,' he replied. 'That was a cheap trick of Fauna's. You okay?' He wrapped his sticky little fingers around hers and tried to pull her up to sit next to him.

'Fauna? It was Fauna that crashed into me!'

'Yes, the little scoundrel. I'll be telling Gus about him, don't you worry.'

'Is that even allowed, to hit someone like that?'

'It most certainly is not. Oh, he'll be in a lot of trouble, you can be certain of that.'

Stella was angry, but also sad. Why did this boy hate her so much?

'Come on,' said Nelson. 'Let's get you back to the treehouse. Shall we walk?'

'Yes please, Nelson. I'd rather not swing for a while.'

Stella took her gloves off and tucked them into her pyjamas. She swung her legs over the side of the net and jumped onto the forest floor.

'I've never loved ground so much,' said Stella, patting it lovingly. She looked up and around at the dark undergrowth. Not much sun reached down here. 'I'm glad you know where you're going.'

'Oh yeah, know this forest like the back of my hand. Also, there are those signs.' Nelson pointed to a sign nailed to a tree that read, "Treehouse this way".

'Oh yes,' said Stella. But still she was glad she had the frog for company as they walked on. 'The Council will think they made a mistake choosing me now.'

'Never. They know you're perfect for this, you and your sister.' And just at that moment, down crashed Dot right next to them, her pyjamas ripped and her hair full of leaves.

'There you are!' she said. 'I was so worried, what happened?'

'Fauna knocked her off her vine, sent her spinning and then her vine snapped in half and dropped her into a net,' said Nelson angrily.

'Uhhh! That horrible boy!'

Stella looked at her dishevelled sister. 'How are you doing, Dot? You look like you've had a fight with a tree.'

'Oh, I'm fine! Really enjoying myself. Pyjamas got in the way so I yanked the sleeves and bottom bits off.'

'Fair enough,' Stella replied wearily. She didn't have the energy to worry about her mum's reaction to ripped pyjamas right now.

Just then Flora swung into view and jumped to the ground in front of them.

'Stella! Are you all right?'

'I'm fine.'

'No thanks to your brother, Flora,' said Nelson.

'Brother!' said Stella and Dot.

'Oh no, what did he do?'

Nelson filled her in.

'I'm so sorry,' said Flora, hanging her head.

'I didn't know he was your brother, Flora.'

'I'm sorry,' she said again. 'He's so difficult, sometimes I wish he wasn't.'

'What he did was really dangerous,' said Stella. 'I thought it was supposed to be a friendly game. A friendly planet for that matter.'

'It is! It really is.' Flora sighed. 'I should tell you everything. Fauna wanted your job; he wanted to captain the *Salvager* and go and rescue animals.'

'Ohhhhhhh,' said Dot.

'So why didn't he?' asked Stella.

'Because of the way he is. He's got a temper and he doesn't always think straight. He loves the animals so much and please believe me, he has a good heart. He's just hurt that he didn't get enough votes.'

'And he's taking it out on me,' said Stella.

'Yes,' said Flora, 'it looks that way. Please don't change

your mind, the animals really need you. We really need you.'

'I won't let him stop me,' said Stella. 'But he needs to understand that we're on the same team. We need to talk.'

'Absolutely. We'll sit down with him as soon as we get back.'

Just then there was a rustling from behind the trees in front of them. Something was coming towards them.

'You're sure all the jaguars are friendly, right?' asked Stella.

But what came out of the undergrowth was more surprising than a jaguar. It was an adult human. He was barefoot, tall and slim with a big, dark, bushy beard.

'Flora,' said the man.

'Dad!' Flora replied and ran to give him a hug.

'Umm, what?' said Dot.

'I didn't think grown-ups were allowed here!' said Stella. She was starting to really dislike all these surprises.

'Not new grown-ups.' The man smiled. 'But old Council members are allowed to stay.'

'Both Mum and Dad were on the Council when they were children, but they stepped down like everyone has to when they turned seventeen,' said Flora. 'We all think that the future of the planet is better governed by children. But all the old Council members still live in the trees with us and help with all the chores. It's just that we make the decisions.'

'It's a pleasure to meet you Stella, Dot. My name is Tracker.' He knelt down in front of the girls and raised the palm of his hand. Stella somehow knew what was expected and she put the palm of her hand against his. Tracker smiled.

Dot came and placed her hand on theirs.

'I am so sorry about my son. It was the wrong thing to do and I promise the Council will make sure he apologises when we find him.'

'Find him?' said the girls.

'Where is he, Dad?' asked Flora worriedly.

'News of what Fauna did reached the treehouse before he did. Gus was very disappointed and Fauna was upset. He took off. We're looking for him now.'

'I hope he's all right,' said Stella.

'I don't,' said Dot.

'He'll be fine, he knows these forests very well.' Tracker turned to Stella. 'He's a good boy really, just too passionate about animals sometimes.'

Stella looked at Tracker and thought of her dad. He'd probably say the same about her.

Tracker continued, 'Flora, you get the girls back to the treehouse. Gus wants to get them home soon.' He turned to the girls. 'Thank you, dear friends. Safe travels.' He ran his hand over his daughter's spiky hair, walked away and disappeared into the forest.

'Are you worried about Fauna?' Stella asked Flora.

'Not really, he can look after himself. He'll come back when he's calmed down.'

The group entered a clearing with nets above their heads and there in front of them rose the mighty treehouse.

'Home!' said Flora.

'Time for a nice cup of tea before we take off I think, girls,' said Nelson, licking his lips.

Flora led the group to a large wooden crate at the foot of the tree that had ropes attached to the corners.

'Jump in,' she said, and blew a horn. The box lurched up and the group looked out over the trees; everything becoming lighter and hotter the higher they got. After a little while they reached the deck. It was packed with children and animals. The noise of everyone clapping, whistling and discussing the game was deafening.

'Girls!' shouted Gus and the girls hugged their feathery friend. 'You were wonderful! I'm so sorry about what Fauna did, Stella.'

'It's all right, I'm fine.'

'It's not fine and he will apologise.'

Stella looked around for River but couldn't see him. She spotted Skyla and Lark's blue faces. They were sitting on the deck a little way off talking and looking at her angrily. She took a deep breath and walked towards them. 'Where's your friend?' she asked.

Skyla was small and lean; her hair was matted and her brown eyes fixed Stella with a piercing glare. Stella held her gaze, refusing to blink. Eventually Skyla smirked unpleasantly. 'I don't know,' she said, looking away. Stella noticed a mark on Skyla's inner arm. It looked like the letter "B". She looked at Lark, he had the same mark. Flora joined the group. 'Are you okay, Stella?'

'I'm fine,' she replied, still looking at Skyla and Lark.

'Don't think everyone here thinks you're amazing just because Flora and gusty bum Gus do,' said Lark and Skyla laughed.

'Stop it. Both of you.' Flora narrowed her eyes at them. 'It's majority rules, Lark, and most of us knew Fauna wasn't right for the job. Something he's just proved today. Come on, Stella.' Stella took a last look at the two council members who clearly didn't like her. She wondered how many more there were.

'Don't let them get you down, Stella, they're harmless. You are always welcome here – look!' A long line of children and animals waited to hug Stella and Dot goodbye.

'Come back, won't you?' said Bramble.

'Of course,' smiled Stella. 'I won't stop thinking about it.'

'Gus,' said Flora, 'is it possible to take a scenic route home for the girls? It would be lovely if they could see some of the work we've done.'

Gus looked at the girls. 'Would you like to see another part of Bea, or shall we just get you home?'

'I'd like to see some more,' said Dot.

'Yes, go on then, that would be nice,' said Stella.

'Excellent,' said Gus. 'A little flight over the tundra then.'

Chapter Five

The balloon had changed colour from a sparkly midnight blue to bright rainbow stripes. Gus smiled at the girls' faces full of wonder. 'The balloon's very creative,' he said.

The *Salvager* gathered speed over the forest until the trees started to thin and all they could see was a vast, flat and treeless land. The girls wrapped themselves in their blankets as the air got cooler and snow appeared below.

And then…the most terrifying noise! Was it a roar? Or a trumpet? Whatever it was, they jumped out of their skins!

'What was that?' Dot whispered.

'That,' replied Gus, 'is a woolly mammoth.' And then they saw it on the horizon as the ship started to slow. It looked like an elephant from a distance but the closer they got they saw its long, curved tusks and black hair, and a hump on his back!

'A woolly mammoth!' Stella repeated in amazement. 'But they're extinct.' It was all still hard to believe.

'One of the proudest and happiest days of my life was bringing them here ten thousand years ago,' said Gus with a tear in his eye.

'Just how old are you?' asked Stella.

'That's a story for another time.' Gus smiled. 'But back to our dear woolly mammoth, look at all his descendants!' The little bird opened his wing in a sweeping gesture and nodded below. The girls looked and saw hundreds of beautiful woolly mammoths walking slowly towards them.

'Helloooooooo!' bellowed one of the magnificent mammals.

'Hello!' cried the girls. 'It's so wonderful to meet you!'

'My name is Walter, with whom do I have the pleasure of speaking? And hello there, Gus!'

'I'm Stella.'

'And I'm Dot.' The girls could not believe what they were seeing, or hearing! They were more excited than the night before Christmas, times a billion.

'Lovely to meet you both. You are in very good company,' said Walter, smiling at his feathery friend.

'It's so amazing to see you! Everyone on Earth thinks you're extinct,' said Stella.

'Yes,' said Walter. 'Probably for the best.'

'Hello!' a small woolly mammoth came running towards them. He tripped over his foot and skidded to a halt on his trunk.

'Oh, Smudge, are you all right, darling?' Walter nudged the young woolly mammoth up with his trunk.

'Yes, Daddy.' The young woolly mammoth gave a shy laugh.

'This is my son, Smudge,' introduced Walter.

'Hi, Smudge!' chorused the girls.

'Do you want to come and play?' asked Smudge.

'Hold on, Smudge, the girls have just got here, they might not want to get trampled by a little woolly mammoth like you.'

'I'd be super careful, I really promise. A lot.'

'Please, Gus! Can we? Can we, Stella?' begged Dot.

Stella and Gus looked at each other. Stella thought

about it and then nodded. 'Sure, Dot.' The thought of spending time with some real life woolly mammoths was too good to pass up.

'Yayyyyy!' shouted Dot and Smudge. Gus gave the command to land.

The *Salvager* lowered to the ground with a gentle bump, the plank went over the side and the girls followed Gus onto the frozen grasses of the tundra. Slowly the herd of woolly mammoths walked towards them.

'Hi, I'm Dot,' said Dot moving towards Smudge.

'Hi,' replied Smudge. 'You look cold.'

'I am a bit.'

'Would you like a cuddle?'

Dot looked at Stella for approval and her sister smiled. Dot walked up to Smudge and put her arms around the baby woolly mammoth, his long dark hair was coarse but warm. Smudge wrapped his trunk around Dot.

'We're going in search of dinner, there are some delicious grasses up ahead, would you like to jump on and come for a stroll?' asked Walter.

'Yes please!' shouted Dot.

'Can we, Gus?' asked Stella.

'Absolutely, girls,' replied the bird. 'Froggies, float the boat alongside, will you?'

Walter lowered his trunk and Stella climbed up, careful not to hurt the beautiful animal.

'Come on, Dot, climb up with me, you're too big for Smudge.' Smudge looked disappointed.

'I'll grow really big one day, then I'll carry you all over Bea, Dot!'

'Thanks, Smudge.' Dot stroked Smudge's trunk and he

tickled her with it. She laughed and then climbed up Walter's trunk.

'Are you ready, girls?' he asked.

Stella gently took handfuls of his hair in her hands and said, 'Ready, Walter!' Walter started to walk, and the girls had a rush of excitement, Walter was so big and strong. They rocked backwards and forwards as his feet flattened the earth below him. They took in their surroundings. There were no trees, only low-lying plants and wildflowers. Large boulders and icy patches of earth were scattered around and the wind whipped the air. Smudge ran alongside them, skidding and jumping with joy. Dot looked behind her and saw the whole herd following close behind. 'You're phenomenal!' she shouted to them. They lifted their trunks and trumpeted an overjoyed reply, 'Aaoooooooooohhhhhh!' The noise roared across the plains. Dot and Stella shrieked with joy.

After a little while the *Salvager* drew alongside Walter and the girls thought they should ask some questions before they had to leave.

'So, do you love Planet Bea?' Dot asked Walter.

'Is it like where you used to live on Earth?' asked Stella.

'It's terrific,' replied Walter. 'This part is called the tundra. It's very much like where we used to live on Earth in what was known as the Ice Age I believe.'

'Why couldn't you live there anymore?' asked Dot.

'Sadly temperatures got warmer on Earth very quickly when my ancestors were there. That changed the amount of rain that fell so that then there weren't as many plants and they didn't have enough to eat. My ancestors were hunted a lot as well,' said Walter sadly. 'We were going to become extinct until Gus rescued us.'

'What does extinct actually mean?' asked Dot. 'It keeps popping up and I've no idea what anyone's on about.'

'It's when an entire species or type of animal all die. They vanish from Earth,' said Walter.

'Oh no! That's just awful!'

'But Gus saved them,' said Stella quietly, as she looked fondly at the little bird sitting in the crow's nest.

'He did.' Walter smiled. 'And a wonderful life we have here too.'

The little bird blushed and the girls thought he was even lovelier than before.

'Oh yum, look at these fabulous grasses!' he came to a halt and turned around to face the herd. 'Dinner, everyone!' Dot and Stella slid down his trunk and into the grass. Smudge was pulling the grass out from its root and shoving it in his mouth.

'Zhissss is wreallyy guuddd,' he mumbled through a mouthful.

'Time we got you home, girls,' said Gus.

Stella hugged Walter's front leg and he patted her with his trunk.

'It was the best meeting you, Walter,' she said.

'The pleasure was all mine, dear. Come and visit us whenever you want.'

'We will.'

Stella and Dot gave Smudge a big hug.

'Come back and play soon, won't you?' said Smudge. 'The council have an awesome game that they play here on stilts! I move the goals!'

'Can't wait!' Shouted Dot jumping up and down.

'Ohhh, great!' said Stella, not sure if it was.

Stella steered Dot up the ship's plank.

'Goodbye, girls,' said Walter.

'Goodbye,' shouted the girls. 'See you soon!'

'Now we really must get you home before you're missed,' said Gus and led them to the captain's cabin as the frogs flew the *Salvager* higher and higher above the tundra and up, up into the sky.

Inside the captain's cabin, Dot climbed onto a window seat and lay down. Stella tucked a blanket around her and she fell instantly asleep. Stella kissed her head and went to join Gus who was sitting around a grand table, the legs of which were carved into waves and mermaids. She pulled one of the heavy wooden chairs out and slumped down into it, dust escaping from its cushion. Candle lit lanterns dimly displayed the dark wooden room's panels.

Stella looked around and saw two maps, one of Earth and one of the solar system. In between them a face was carved into the wooden wall of the ship. As exhausted as she was, she was drawn to it. She walked over to the face and ran her finger over it. It was a girl a little older than Stella, with long curly hair. Her left hand touched her right shoulder and the top of her dress was old-fashioned with a bodice and puffy sleeves. Stella looked at her lovely face; she looked so sad.

'Beatrice.' Stella jumped at the sound of Gus's voice.

'This is Beatrice,' whispered Stella. She couldn't take her eyes off the wooden face. 'Who is she?'

'She was the daughter of a pirate, 350 years ago.' Stella breathed in sharply, she didn't want to believe this girl was gone, she felt like she knew her.

'What happened to her?'

'She couldn't stand the sailors hunting animals anymore. She knew a species of bird was dying out on an island called Mauritius. She felt their pain. So, with some of the local children's help she stole her father's ship and I flew the remaining birds to a planet I had found.'

'What was the bird?' Stella turned to Gus.

'The dodo,' he replied, smiling.

'She saved the dodo!'

'Yes. They joined the woolly mammoths and other animals that I had brought here many years prior. Now they live on a volcanic island on Bea surrounded by coral reefs. I'll take you there one day if you'd like to meet them?'

'I'd love to,' replied Stella. 'And Beatrice?' Gus looked wistful.

'Land ahoy!' came a shout from one of the frogs on the deck.

'Another time,' said Gus, patting her hand with his wing.

Stella rubbed her eyes to stop a tear from forming and went over to her sister. She looked out of the window as Earth came into view. It was breath-taking, clouds swirled over the top of emerald greens, sapphire blues and ochre browns. She was suddenly very tired. The ship hurtled towards Australia and down to the bottom right-hand corner. Stella gently shook her sister awake as the *Salvager* landed on the roof of their parents' house.

'When will we go back to Bea, Gus?' Stella asked.

'Next week, my dear. There's more I want you to see before you embark on your first mission.'

'You still think we're the best people for the job?'

'Unquestionably, Stella. I know so.'

Stella kissed the bird goodbye and led her sleepy sister to bed. It had been an unbelievable night. She was both happy and sad, nervous and excited. But mainly, she couldn't wait for her next time on Bea.

Chapter Six

Stella sat in her Geography class. For the first time in her life she wasn't listening to a thing her teacher was saying. Instead, she was doodling on her exercise book. She drew four posts with ropes swinging between them.

'Stella? Stella!' Mrs Beard was calling out from the front of the class.

'Yes?' Stella was jolted back to reality.

'I asked you what the word tundra means?'

'A vast, flat, treeless Arctic region of Europe, Asia, and North America in which the subsoil is permanently frozen.'

'Right. Very good.' Mrs Beard looked a little sheepish.

'It's amazing, you should go.'

Mrs Beard couldn't work out whether her usually excellent student was being cheeky. 'Come and see me after class please.'

The class giggled and Stella looked at her best friend, Zara, who gave her a sympathetic smile.

When the bell rang sounding the end of the class Stella slowly packed her backpack while the other children left the room. She walked up to Mrs Beard.

'Is everything okay, Stella? You seem very distracted.'

'I'm fine, thank you,' Stella replied, she wasn't very good at not saying what was on her mind.

'Well if there's something you need help with my door's always open.'

'Thanks, Mrs B.' Stella left the classroom and found Zara waiting for her.

'What did she say?' Zara asked.

'Oh nothing really, said I was distracted.'

'You do seem a bit. What's going on?'

Stella looked her best friend in the eye. She wished she could tell her everything: about Gus and the *Salvager*, space and Planet Bea, Leap Frog and River.

'It's just... it's just exams coming up, bit nervous, that's all.'

'Yikes if you're worried, I should probably have a breakdown.'

Stella smiled at her friend. 'Please don't.' The girls hugged and walked outside to find their bus home.

That night in bed Stella turned to face her sister.

'I found out more about Beatrice. She was a pirate's daughter. She stole her father's ship and rescued dodos!'

'Um, what?'

'I know. Her face is carved into the *Salvager*'s cabin. She was lovely.'

'When was this?'

'350 years ago, Gus said. There's something really sad about it all. About her.'

'Well if you ask me she sounds really cool. Daughter of a pirate! A-mazing. Stole his ship! Brilliant. Saved the dodo! Awesome. I hope I'm remembered for something like that.'

Stella laughed. 'I don't doubt it'll be something crazy like that, Dot.'

Dot smiled. 'Night, Stella.'

'Night, Dot.'

Stella closed her eyes and fell asleep until...*thud,* the now familiar sound of the *Salvager*. The girls weren't startled this time, they just looked at each other and smiled.

'Let's go,' said Stella and led the way up and onto the ship.

As they entered space Dot helped the frogs with their duties on board the ship. Stella watched as she shimmied up the crow's nest and unhooked a sail. The frogs looked impressed.

'And how are you, Stella?' asked Gus who was chewing on a pipe, rainbow coloured smoke escaping from his beak. 'Filthy habit,' he said to Stella who was looking disapproving.

'I'm fine. Although everyone keeps asking me how I am, so maybe I'm not.'

'It's a lot to take in. Perhaps too much? We can go longer between visits if you're tired?'

'No, not tired. Weirdly we never seem to have been gone for long according to the clock so I still get to sleep. I just wish I could tell Mum and Dad really; I just want to share all of these amazing experiences with them.'

'Of course. I completely understand and I'm so sorry that you can't.'

'I understand why not. I'm not sure they'd be too happy about us being in space right now, Dot dangling from a mast,' Stella said with a laugh.

'She's very good at it though, isn't she?' Gus chuckled.

'So what will we do on Bea this time?'

'Well River said that you were keen on foraging with him, is that right?'

Stella swallowed hard. 'Sure.'

'Excellent. Well let's go walkabout then.'

The sky started to lighten.

'Looks like we're nearly home.' And if a beak could smile, it would have.

The ship slowed as it descended through the clouds. Dot reached overboard to touch one and Stella just managed to grab hold of her shirt.

'Oh!' said Dot, disappointed. 'It's not fluffy, it's just a bit damp.'

'There are the council!' shouted Stella as the treehouse and children came into view.

'We're not landing today,' shouted Gus, 'we're just picking people up.'

The girls waved to everyone on the deck. 'Hi Bramble, hi Flora!' shouted Dot.

'Hi girls!' Flora replied.

The frogs threw two ropes over the side of the ship.

'For River and Forest,' said Gus.

'I don't think I've met Forest, have I?' asked Stella.

'No, she had gone bush when you were here last. She likes to get away from the treehouse sometimes, live off the land.'

The frogs were hanging over the side of the ship, pulling the visitors aboard. River climbed over first and jumped onto the deck. He looked up and saw Stella and smiled. Dot ran over to him. 'Hi River, you big Blue Team meanie.' River looked worried. 'Only joking!' Dot laughed and River looked relieved, but searched Stella's face to see if she was cross too.

'I didn't see you after the game,' Stella said.

'I'd gone to look for Fauna. I was really angry with him for what he did to you.'

'Thanks.' Stella felt instantly relieved that River didn't dislike her, he was actually on her side. 'Did you find him?'

'No. No one has.' Now she was worried again.

'He's still missing?'

'Yes.' River looked concerned.

Stella hoped he was okay. 'He'll be all right,' she said bravely, trying to hide her own worry.

A girl climbed over the side of the *Salvager*. 'This is Forest,' introduced River, 'she knows the area we're going to really well.' Forest walked towards Stella. She wore dungarees similar to the others, but she had a shirt underneath that covered her arms. She raised the palm of her hand to Stella and then Dot, both girls touching her hand as was the tradition. Forest had dark skin and long black braids with feathers hanging from the ends.

'Ooh you're so pretty!' announced Dot.

'Dot!' said Stella and shook her head.

'What?'

'Thank you,' said Forest and she turned to Stella and looked her straight in the eyes. It was such a strong gaze that Stella felt dizzy. There was something powerful about her.

'It's good to finally put a face to your name, Stella. Everyone's certainly been talking a lot about you.'

Stella tried to read her expression. She wasn't sure if she meant they'd been saying good or bad things.

'Where are we going?' asked Dot.

Forest looked at Stella for an uncomfortable second longer, and then turned to Dot. 'There's a large part of Bea that's just like your bushland in Australia.' She offered Dot her hand. 'Come, I'll show you.'

Forest and Dot walked over to the crow's nest and Forest started to climb. She was very graceful and incredibly fast.

'Hold on, I'll come too!' shouted Stella but Dot was already hot on Forest's heels. Stella followed the girls, carefully placing her feet on the rungs of the pole and pulling herself up by her hands. One foot slipped off and she hugged the pole tight. Where were her Leap Frog gloves when she needed them? She looked down at Gus and River who now seemed tiny and then back up at the crow's nest; Forest and Dot were safely inside. She climbed up and through the hatch. Dot moved over and Stella stood up, clutching onto the side. She was starting to realise she really didn't like heights.

But then she saw the view.

They had flown in a different direction to the last time when they had met Walter in the tundra. The midday sun would have been scorching where they were now but the afternoon sun felt good on their skin, the light was soft and everything glowed orange. A warm wind blew through the girls' hair and they were bursting with happiness.

'Wahoooooooooooo!' shouted Dot.

'Yeaahhhhhhhh!' sang Stella. Forest looked at them and laughed, Stella hoped they could be friends.

After a while, the tall trees packed in closely next to each other started to thin. The landscape was changing from rainforest to wide open spaces and then sandstone mountains, steep rocky walls, waterfalls and gorges. The trees were eucalyptus and the rolling hills were scattered with shrubs and wildflowers.

'Here!' shouted Forest down to Gus. 'I can see a clearing; we can land there.'

The frogs leapt into action, overboard went the anchor and down went the ship. Stella, Dot and Forest climbed down from the crow's nest and joined Gus and River looking out at the landscape.

The weather was warm and the sky was the bluest of blues. The sun's rays shone on the bright orange earth and the bluey grey bark of the gum trees. The air was so fresh and still, all you could hear were the birds and the insects and all you could smell was the eucalyptus.

'It's beautiful here,' said Stella.

'So like home!' said Dot, skipping down the plank.

'Why don't you have a walk around, I'll make camp for the night,' said Forest. 'There's a stream over there if you want to fill up some water bottles.'

She pointed to behind the ship, the light illuminating her shirt sleeves. Stella remembered the "B" symbol on Lark and Skyla's forearms and wondered if Forest had one too.

'Shall we?' said River, smiling to Stella and Stella beamed back.

'Ugh, I think I'll stay here,' said Dot, pretending to be sick.

Stella and River got the bottles from the ship and walked off in search of the stream. The ground was dusty and the sun was still strong.

They walked in silence as Stella tried to think of something clever to say.

'Do you hear that?' asked River.

72

'What? Oh yeah – water!'

They followed the sound of the running water walking towards some gumtrees that lined a beautiful stream. The water ran quickly over rocks, cascading down small waterfalls and eventually winding off around a corner in the distance. They walked to the water's edge and filled their bottles with water.

River was looking off absent-mindedly at the other side of the stream and Stella splashed him.

'Hey!' he said, laughing, and splashed her back. They sat back under the shade of a tree.

Stella turned to River, 'Why do Skyla and Lark have the letter "B" on their arms?'

'Oh that.' River rolled his eyes. 'So stupid of them. We've all grown up hearing about Beatrice and her time on Mauritius. The legend goes that the children there came up with a way of finding out who knew about Beatrice's mission to save the dodos, who could be trusted. They would draw a line in the sand and if another child drew a wave next to it to make the letter B then they knew they were part of the group. It's always been a favourite story of children on Bea, we grew up playing games where some of us would pretend to be on team Beatrice and some on team Grownup.'

'But Skyla and Lark aren't playing a game now?'

'No. Recently when Fauna wasn't voted in as captain of the *Salvager,* he and a few of his stupid friends started writing the letter B on their arms.'

'So they're saying their allegiance is with Beatrice, rather than me,' Stella stated.

'Yes. But don't worry about them. You can't please

everyone right?'

'I'm not trying to replace her.'

'I know. They're idiots, don't worry about them. None of them could do as good a job as you.'

'I really don't know that for sure. Neither do you.'

'Yeah, I do.' River smiled.

'So are you going to show me how you forage?'

'Sure!'

They stood up and brushed the dirt off themselves. Stella led the way. 'It's so like Australia, I can't believe it.'

'Well, you'll probably recognize what you can eat then?'

'Maybe! Well, over there – that's finger lime, isn't it?'

'Yes!' They walked over to a thorny shrub with long green fruit that looked like fingers. Stella snapped it in half, revealing lots of small, pinkish-white beads.

'It is okay, isn't it?' she asked.

'It's fine, go for it.'

River took one of the fruits too and they both sucked the delicious tangy citrus pulp out of them.

'So good!' said Stella. They wiped their mouths with the back of their hands and kept walking.

'Oh look,' said River, 'Lilly Pilly!' they walked over to a tall bush with dark green leaves and dark red berries.

'We have these in our garden,' said Stella, picking a couple of the berries and popping them in her mouth. 'Oh, so sour!' Her face screwed up as she tried to swallow the tart fruit.

'Better when cooked.' River laughed as Stella stuck her tongue out and closed her eyes in mock disgust. They walked back to the *Salvager* giggling. When they got back to the camp it was almost dark. Forest had made a fire and River taught Stella how to make damper bread which they baked on the hot coals. After they'd eaten, everyone lay back and watched the stars while Forest told them stories of how the universe came to be and how the creator intended for humans to live within the world as they knew it.

When Forest finished everyone was full of wonder and ready to dream incredible dreams.

'Goodnight, everyone,' said Gus.

'Goodnight,' croaked the frogs.

Stella looked over at River and he smiled and mouthed goodnight to her. She lay down next to Dot and zipped the swag up around them, smiling blissfully to herself.

'You're weird,' said Dot.

'Fine,' replied Stella, still smiling.

Stella woke with a start. She unzipped her swag and climbed out, making sure Dot was zipped safely back in. Everyone in the camp was still sleeping but she had a feeling something wasn't right. The air hummed with mosquitoes. River was asleep but Forest's swag was empty. The moon was bright and lit everything in the clearing of the camp but the bush around them was pitch black. A twig snapped. Something was out there.

'Forest?' she called. 'Is that you?'

Nothing. She plucked up all her courage and walked towards the bush. She wasn't going to let anything hurt her sister. She stepped into the bush, her eyes trying to focus on the shadows.

'Who's there?' she called. 'I'm a friend, I won't hurt you.'

And then he moved out from behind a tree.

'Fauna,' she said. He was even dirtier than before, covered in mud and scratches: he had never looked so wild.

Fauna walked quickly towards her. The moon lit up his face and showed the anger in his eyes. 'Hello, Stella.' Stella walked backwards, trying to keep some distance between them, but tripped and fell to the ground.

'What are you doing here?' she asked.

'Well, I can't go home. You've seen to that.' Stella tried to stay calm; she knew panicking would not help but she could tell the boy wanted to fight. 'And I can't go and save any animals because…you took my job.'

'I didn't take your job. The Council gave it to me.' She was scared of Fauna now.

'The Council!' said Fauna, a look of disgust on his face. 'I'm so sick of the Council. Why do they get to decide? I love animals just as much as them, if not more.'

'I know. Flora told me.'

'She did?' his face softened ever so slightly.

'Yes. She said you have a big heart.' Fauna looked away, ashamed. Stella hoped she was getting through to him and kept going. 'And I met your dad.'

'Tracker!' Now Fauna was really interested. 'What did he say?' Stella started to get to her feet, but Fauna pushed her back onto the ground. 'What did my dad say?' he said through gritted teeth.

A strange noise came from the bush, like an animal call. *Coo coooo. Coo Coooooooo.* 'What's that?' asked Fauna.

'I, I don't know,' said Stella. 'You don't know either?'

'I don't live in this part of the planet.' The noise grew louder: *coo coooo coo cooooo.* 'What did my dad say!'

'He said you're a good boy and that you care so much about Bea and the animals.'

'I do! He won't think I'm a good boy now.' He kicked a stone. 'Get up, let's move away from that noise, I don't like it.' Fauna grabbed Stella's hand and pulled her up roughly.

Stella didn't want to go anywhere with Fauna but she did want to get him away from Dot. They walked through the bush, Stella in front and Fauna behind. The strange noise only got louder. *Coo cooooo*. Stella tried to keep Fauna talking.

'I'm sorry I took your job. I thought I was helping. You know we want the same thing, me and you, we just want what's best for the animals.' Fauna didn't say anything and it made Stella more nervous, she wanted to hear him talk, to try and make things less hostile. 'Gus told me about Beatrice.'

'You're nothing compared to her.'

'I know, I'm not trying to compete. I know I could never replace her or what she means to you all. And I know about the B symbol on Skyla and Lark's arms.'

'They're loyal to me.'

'Oh yes, I really know that. They made that very clear.' Stella tried to think quickly, what could she say that would make him calm down? 'Listen, I'm not trying to be in charge around here, I just want to help. You all know much more about the planet and the animals here, about your incredible history. I've got lots to learn from you.'

'Yeah, you do.'

'So teach me! Tell me about Bea and what you do here. If River's a forager, what's your job?'

'I make things, things you never could!'

'I don't doubt it. Tell me about them.'

'What's the point? I'll never be able to go back now.'

'Course you can, I'm not going to stop you. I know everyone's worried about you. Believe it or not I was, too.'

There was a silence that seemed to last forever. Occasionally a cloud would cover the moon and she was walking blindly through the grasses and shrubs. She could hear Fauna still walking behind her and eventually he spoke.

'I make things. I'm really good at making things.'

'Like what?' she tried to sound calm and not scared.

'Like the lift that gets you up to the top of the treehouse. I built that.'

'I've been in it, it's great! Well done.'

'And the tank that collects the rainwater. Oh, and the draw bridge! Have you seen it? It's really cool.'

'No, I haven't.' Stella turned her head around. 'It sounds it.' She could see Fauna's face, his features looked frozen in horror. Stella followed his gaze down to his feet and saw a snake.

'Nice and calm,' she said softly, 'don't move.' She walked slowly to the snake and it turned around to face her.

'Are you okay, Sssstelllaa?' it asked.

'Hi,' Stella replied. 'Yes, yes I'm fine, thank you.'

The snake turned back to Fauna and hissed. 'Sssssstella is here to help animals, Fauna. I will protect Sssstellla.'

'That's very kind of you and I really appreciate it,' said Stella to the snake, 'but there's no need to hurt Fauna.'

The snake's muscular body rose and he opened his mouth and hissed at Fauna.

'Stop, friend, please,' said Stella desperately. 'I'm sorry, I don't know your name?'

'I'm Ssssimon,' hissed the snake. 'I have heard of you and your ssssisssster and how you want to help. I have relatives on Earth that need ssssaving.'

'Well, it's a pleasure to meet you. And I will absolutely do my best. Now please let Fauna go.'

Simon looked at Stella and lowered his head to the ground but just then, *COO COOOOO*! The noise was practically on top of them. Fauna jumped and looked up at the trees. He lost his footing and reached out for something to grab. The clouds cleared and the sudden light showed a huge cliff drop. Fauna wobbled on the edge; Stella ran towards him and caught the boy's hand, his terrified face stared into hers. She pulled with all her strength and they fell back onto the ground, small rocks toppling over the cliff edge.

'Are you all right?' she asked, trying to catch her breath. Fauna shook with fear, his eyes looked as though they would burst. She hugged him as his chest rose with sobs.

'I'm sorry, I'm sorry.'

'Never mind,' she said, trying to stop her heart from racing.

'Fauna! What have you done?' Stella and Fauna looked up from the ground; Tracker and Forest were standing in front of them.

'Dad!' Fauna got to his feet and ran to his father. Tracker held him and then dropped onto his knees, holding Fauna at arm's length.

Forest ran over to Stella. 'Stella!' She helped her to her feet, and checked for any injuries.

'I'm fine,' said Stella, hoping she was. 'What are you both doing here?'

Tracker spoke first, 'I've been looking for Fauna since you left,' he looked at Fauna. 'I was worried about you, son.' Fauna looked ashamed. 'I knew I was close to finding him, and then I heard Forest's warning call.'

'That's what that was?' said Stella.

Forest explained, 'I couldn't sleep so I went for a walk and found Tracker, who told me he'd found Fauna's footprints. I left Tracker looking for him and headed back to the camp. And then I saw you and Fauna and I saw him push you to the ground. I sent out a warning call to Tracker for help.'

'I'm sorry I didn't get here sooner,' said Tracker. 'But it looks like you handled it, Stella.'

'She sssssaved him,' said Simon, who had slithered in front of Stella protectively. 'She ssssstopped him from falling off the cliff.' Fauna hung his head and cried.

'Thank you,' said Tracker to Stella, 'with all my heart.' He turned to his son. 'You owe Stella a big apology, Fauna.' Fauna looked at the ground. 'Fauna!' Tracker repeated.

Fauna looked up at Stella, his face remorseful.

'You hurt me, Fauna. You scared me,' Stella said to the boy softly.

'Sorry,' Fauna mumbled, looking down at the ground.

'I just want you to understand that I'm on your side. I'm not the enemy. We all want the same thing.'

Fauna nodded his head. 'Sorry I scared you. And like, swung into you.'

It wasn't a very convincing apology but Stella knew it was all she was likely to get right then and all she really wanted was to sit down. Forest crouched down next to her.

Stella looked at her. 'Thanks for trying to help me.'

'Of course!'

'I thought you might have been on Fauna's side?'

'Why?'

'You just seemed a little distant and, well, I thought you might have a "B" on your arm.'

'A "B"? As in team Beatrice? No.' She rolled up her sleeves, showing no marks. 'I'm just sensible, I keep the sun off me during the day and I keep warm at night.' She smiled. 'And I'm sorry if I was distant, I just wanted to see for myself what you were like.'

'And?'

'And you're good.' The girls smiled. 'You want to start over?'

'Sure. Can we start by you helping me up? My legs are like jelly.'

River gently woke Stella at first light. 'Hi there, hero.' He smiled. The events of the night came flooding back to her.

'Hi. Not sure about the hero.' She felt like she could sleep for another few days but slowly sat up.

'This isn't what I wanted you to experience on Bea, it's not normally like this. I'm getting a bit worried you might not come back.'

'I'll come back,' she said, getting to her feet. 'Where's Dot?'

'Making Fauna feel really bad. She has my blessing.' Stella looked around the camp which was being packed away by the frogs and saw Dot and Gus standing over a miserable looking Fauna who was sitting on the ground.

Stella and River walked towards them, she looked at Fauna's face pleading for Dot to stop telling him off and she actually felt sorry for him.

'Stella!' Dot jumped on her sister and gave her a hug. 'Forest told me what happened and now this very naughty boy is getting a piece of my mind.'

'Lots of pieces,' said Fauna.

'How are you, dear one? I shan't let you out of my sight again,' said Gus, holding her tight.

'I'm fine, really.' She tried to look reassuring. 'But maybe it's time to go home.'

'Agreed,' said Gus. 'Froggies!'

Stella, Dot, River, Forest, Fauna and Tracker climbed onboard the *Salvager* and Gus flew up to the crow's nest and ignited its wick. A little gust of wind trumpeted from his tail feathers and, had it been possible for feathers to turn pink, they would have done so. The frogs rolled their eyes and sailed the ship up and over the gum trees.

Stella and River watched as the morning sun rose over the planet.

'I was wondering if ummm...' River looked awkward, Gus refused to leave Stella's side, 'if maybe you wanted to come with me foraging again the next time you're here?'

Stella looked out at the majestic scenery. 'That would be nice.'

The ship arrived at the treehouse and hovered over the deck. A horn blared to signal their arrival and all the children ran out to see them.

Stella and River gave each other an awkward hug.

'See you soon, then,' said River.

'See you soon,' replied Stella. She was proud of herself

for all that she'd achieved. Forest came to say goodbye and she gave her a hug. 'Bye, Forest.'

'Thanks Stella, for everything you've done. You're just what this place needs, you and your sister.' Dot hugged Forest tightly.

River and Forest picked up ropes and jumped off the ship and down onto the deck.

Tracker came to say goodbye. 'Thank you again, Stella. Fauna's learnt a valuable lesson, haven't you son?'

'Yes, Dad.' Fauna rolled his eyes. Dot gave him a little kick.

'Ow!'

'Take care, both of you,' said Tracker to the sisters.

'See you soon, Fauna,' said Stella.

'Bye,' said Fauna and climbed over the side of the ship with his rope. 'We could always have another game of Leap Frog when you come back. I'll let you win next time.'

'Let me win?' Stella laughed. 'I was beating you!'

Fauna half smiled. 'Whatever,' he said and he disappeared over the side of the ship. Stella shook her head.

'Can I please start getting off the ship like that?' asked Dot excitedly.

'Perhaps soon, Dot.' Gus jumped up onto her shoulder with a smile and they went to join the frogs in sailing the ship back to Earth.

But there was something Stella couldn't stop thinking about. She walked through the hold of the ship and to the door of the captain's cabin. She slowly turned the handle of the heavy wooden door.

She pushed the door open and walked into the room. A sudden breeze made her shiver. She walked over to the carving of Beatrice and held out her hand to touch her face. 'What happened to you?' she asked quietly. All of the emotion of the night before hit her like a train and she slumped on the floor beneath the wooden panel and cried into her bent knees until she fell asleep.

She opened her eyes to see Gus talking to a girl with long curly hair wearing a dress with a bodice. She walked around the table to look at her face and realised it was Beatrice.

'I have to stay, Gus,' Beatrice said to the bird. 'It's the only way you can all escape.'

Gus pleaded with the girl. 'If they think you had something to do with the ship leaving, your father won't be able to protect you, Beatrice, his men will be too strong.'

'That's a risk I'm going to have to take.' The girl spun around on her heels and walked towards Stella and then right through her. A chill flooded Stella's body, she turned to see Beatrice walk out through the door of the cabin.

'Beatrice!' Gus's voice screeched in Stella's ears.

'Stella, Stella.' Gus was shaking her gently with his wing. 'Stella dear, wake up.'

'Oh Gus! I saw you. And Beatrice. You were telling her not to leave, that her father couldn't protect her!'

'What? You saw that in your sleep?'

'Yes, you were right here, in this room.'

Gus looked up at the carving of Beatrice. 'The ship is powerful. It has a memory of her.'

'What happened to her, Gus? I have to know.'

The little bird sighed. 'Yes, you do.' He hopped up into a chair and slumped down into it. Stella stayed frozen to the spot in front of the carving of Beatrice, she didn't dare even breathe until she'd heard the story.

'It was 1662. Beatrice's father was the feared Pirate Catanzo and this was his ship. He and his men had docked it off Mauritius for several months. Beatrice had made many trips to the island and had become friends with a lot of the children there. They told her of their beloved native bird and how they feared for its extinction. So many were hunted. I had heard of their plight too and feared the same. That's why I was on the island, and that's how I met her.

'Together we hatched a plan to save the birds. A great feast was planned for Pirate Catanzo and his men on Mauritius, and Beatrice decided it was the perfect time to smuggle the endangered birds and the children who wanted to protect them from the island. While the men were eating, she helped the birds and children aboard the dinghy and told them to row to the ship. The children didn't want to leave without her, but she made them, she said someone needed to stay behind so they didn't blame the other children on the island.

'When the children and the birds arrived at the ship it took all my powers to lift it up out of the ocean and fly it to the planet I had found. The planet didn't have a name then, I just called it Planet B as Earth was Planet A and it wasn't working as I had hoped.

'My power wasn't as strong then and I struggled to carry the ship. When I tried to land the ship at Planet B I couldn't carry it any further and it crashed into the forest. The ship's sails were damaged beyond repair. It took me and the children many months to build the balloon and create the ship as we know it today. We named it the *Salvager* as it means to rescue or save something. All along we were so happy we had saved the birds and they were making a new home for themselves, but we were so worried about Beatrice. By the time we had built the new ship and I flew it back to Earth and to Mauritius…'

'Yes?'

'She was gone.'

'Gone? Gone where?'

'I don't know. I couldn't find her, or her father, and no one wanted to talk about them. Pirate Catanzo was a bad man. But he loved his daughter, that's why he had had this carving of her made. He wanted to show her the world and for her to become a pirate. But she was different, she cared about people and animals. I prayed every day that she was safe but I never saw her again. She sacrificed herself for the birds and the children, and for her father too.'

'Poor Beatrice.'

'Yes. When I finally gave up searching for her, I returned to the planet and the children and we renamed it Planet Beatrice. We vowed to rescue as many animals as we could for her.'

'And I will too,' said Stella, touching the wooden face again.

'You know, you look like her,' said Gus.

'I think maybe I do.' Stella turned and smiled at Gus. 'I'll try to make her proud.'

'I'm sure you already have, dear girl.'

Chapter Seven

Mallacoota, Victoria, Australia.

Pella the koala raised her nose to the air. She could smell fire. Birds were screaming at her and the other animals in the bush to run. Pella climbed up the highest tree and saw fire in the west. She climbed back down as quickly as she could without dropping her joey Nara, who was clinging to her back, and she started to run.

Healesville, Victoria
Sunday 17th November, 1 a.m.

A familiar but still heart-stopping thud sounded on Stella and Dot's bedroom roof.

'It can't be,' said Dot, sitting up in bed. 'It hasn't been a week…'

Gus flapped outside their window and tapped on the glass urgently.

'What is it, what's wrong?' asked Stella as she opened the window.

'It's the bush, it's on fire! Quickly, we've got to help the animals!'

'I'll bring my doctor's bag,' said Stella.

The girls scrambled onto the roof, ran up the plank and onto the *Salvager*. There, standing in a row were River,

Forest and Fauna.

'We've come to help you,' said River.

'You'll know what to do,' said Forest.

'You're the boss,' said Fauna.

'What's happened?' asked Stella.

'There are bushfires all over Australia. Millions of animals are at risk.' Gus had tears in his eyes. 'We've got to get there right away and get them onto the ship.'

'Okay,' said Stella

'Are you ready Stella, are you ready to save animals?'

Stella didn't need to think twice. 'Yes. We'll need water. There's a dam at the back of our house, do we have any buckets?'

'Yes, Stella, lots,' said Nelson.

'Get them ready, I'll show you the way.'

The ship took off and flew over some gum trees at the back of the Peters' property. Stella pointed to the dam and it landed alongside it.

'Everyone, grab a bucket.'

The children ran down the plank and filled the buckets with water and carried them hurriedly back onto the ship.

'They're all full,' said Forest.

'Then let's go!'

The *Salvager* raced through the night until they saw a terrifying glow on the horizon. Kangaroos hopped as fast as they could away from where the ship was headed. They flew closer to the fires, the wind blowing the smoke away from them. The children stared in horror at the amount of land alight. Bright orange and red flames higher than a skyscraper stretched as far as the eye could see and huge billowy clouds of smoke filled the sky, grey and black and menacing. Everything was burning. They thought all the world must be on fire.

'Can we fly through the smoke?' asked Stella.

The little bird replied, 'With this we can!'

They ran to the side of the ship where the frogs were uncovering…a cannon! One frog packed it with silver powder, another pushed the powder down the barrel with a long stick and then the rest of the crew hauled on ropes to pull it to the gunport, a window in the side of the ship.

Gus then opened his mouth, his tummy rumbled and 'poooooooffff', a flame jumped out of his beak and onto the cannon's wick. With a tremendous explosion a strange silvery bubble emerged from the end of the cannon. It grew and it wobbled and bubbled and grew some more. The smoke from the fires had started to surround the ship and everything glowed eerily in the orange light. Dot started to cough and it was hard to see where the silvery bubble had gone until 'POP!' they and the *Salvager* were inside it! Suddenly there was no noise, everything was calm and they could breathe again.

'Phew,' said Gus, 'that's better.' Stella went to the side of the ship and reached out to touch the bubble. It was cool and sticky and smelt of peppermint.

'We're safe in here,' reassured Gus. 'An amazing design, if I say so myself.'

'Doesn't it melt?' asked Dot.

'Oh no. We landed on the sun once and it was fine!'

Through the minty bubble they could see the smoke lit by the fires, swirling and circling the ship. A flock of cockatoos appeared outside the bubble.

'We've got to help them!' shouted Stella. She ran to the

bubble and the birds looked in, confused and terrified. Stella couldn't stand it any longer; she put her hand through the bubble. It oozed around her fingers cold and wet and slimy until she reached the hot air outside. 'Take my hand!' she shouted. The birds saw her hand beckon to them but they couldn't understand what she was saying through the bubble. 'I have to talk to them,' she said to herself. She took a big gulp of air and plunged her head into the wet blubbery bubble. It squelched in her ears, and then her face was slapped with the heat of the fires.

'Take my hand,' she said to the flapping birds, 'it's safe in here.' The birds didn't give it a second thought; they flew onto her arm and she pulled them inside the bubble.

'Quickly, River!' she shouted. 'Get the water.' The birds drank thirstily.

'Are you hurt?' Dot held her sister tight.

'I'm fine. It's awful out there. The poor animals.'

'Prepare to land!' shouted Gus from the crow's nest.

A frog threw the anchor over the side of the ship. It hit the ground and the ship jolted down. The frogs lowered the plank.

'You all stay here,' said Gus. 'I'll go and see if there are any animals outside.'

'I want to come, too,' said Stella.

'Don't go!' cried Dot. 'You'll get hurt!' Tears streamed down her face.

The little bird looked at Stella. 'That is very admirable Stella, but not possible. You will get hurt, possibly worse, and we can't lose you. We need you to treat the animals.'

'What about you?' asked Stella.

'I'll be fine. Nothing can damage these fiery lungs.' He

smiled.

'I'll get my bag ready. Good luck.'

He walked to the top of the plank, waved goodbye and then squeezed through the slimy wall of the bubble. The children ran to the edge to look for him but everything was too blurry and smoky outside.

'Come on,' said Stella, 'let's make ourselves useful.' Stella took out the burn ointment and bandages from her bag. 'See if the frogs have some clean cloths and wet them.'

The children and the frogs sat on the deck ripping sheets into strips and praying that Gus was all right. Every second felt like an hour. And then, 'Look!' said Forest. At the top of the plank a multi-coloured beak poked through the bubble, and then a feathery chest and wings! 'Gus!' they shouted and ran to help.

'Stand back everyone, we have guests!' Through the bubble came some furry paws: a koala! Then two koalas. Then ten, twenty, thirty koalas and a kangaroo too, then more kangaroos! Possums and wombats and echidnas and birds, hundreds of them! There was no time to spare. The frogs showed the animals to the buckets where they gulped down the water. Dot, River, Forest and Fauna wrapped any burns in wet compresses and then Stella applied ointment and bandaged them up. Gus made more and more trips outside, trying to find as many animals as he could.

'He needs help,' said Stella. 'The two of us would find double the animals.'

'No, Stella, you heard what he said,' warned River.

'I have to try.'

'There's no point trying to stop you, is there?' River could tell by her expression. Stella knew it was dangerous but she had to help the animals, it was always the animals. She gave Dot a quick kiss on her head, picked up one of the ropes coiled at the side of the ship, and tied it around her waist.

'So I won't get lost,' she said. 'Fauna, can you hold the other end. If you feel a tug, I might need to be pulled back in.'

'Aye, Captain.'

She wrapped a damp cloth over her nose and mouth and stepped onto the plank and out through the bubble.

Pella the koala couldn't see anything any more, the smoke was too thick. She couldn't hear anything either over the deafening roar of the flames. She held her joey, Nara, and didn't know what to do.

The heat hit Stella as soon as she left the cool bubble wall. She couldn't see further than a few feet away. She walked down the plank and when she reached the earth below, she got down on all fours. She knew she had to stay low, that the freshest air is on the ground. She crawled as fast as she could, feeling the parched earth below her. Pieces of ash flew in the air and she couldn't tell if the dark shapes were animals or shrubs. She saw something small in front of her and moved towards it.

Pella felt a gentle weight on her back. She wondered if this was the end and wrapped herself around her joey to protect her. But the weight had a voice that she could understand. 'Quickly,' it said, 'come with me.'

Stella put her arm around the mother and baby koala and with the other arm tugged the rope. The rope began to pull them in.

Pella could see that it was a human leading them now. A young human by the looks of it. How did she understand what the human had said? She could make out a huge shape with a bright rainbow balloon above it. She didn't know what it was but she knew it was the only chance they had.

She walked onto a plank with the figure guiding her way and suddenly she and Nara squeezed through a cool, wet, sticky goo that smelled like the native mint of the bush. She and her joey's eyes blinked in disbelief as they popped through the sticky wall and onto a huge ship to see hundreds of animals and birds sitting on the floor, frogs tending to their wounds. A little girl ran towards the young human who had saved them and they hugged. The young human took a cloth off from around her face and said, 'Hello, I'm Stella.'

Stella checked on the animals' wounds and told the others what to do before going back outside. She brought more and more animals in, tended to their wounds and went back into the fires again. No one had a chance to stop for a second. The *Salvager* and its silvery bubble took off and landed countless times until it was packed with birds, animals, insects and buckets full of fish.

'We're running out of ointment,' said Dot to Stella.

'Ask Nelson if there's any salt on the ship. Mix it with water to clean their wounds.'

Hours went by and the sun began to rise. Stella saw Gus popping in through the bubble. 'There's no room left on the ship.'

'Then we'll have to take them to Planet Bea and come back.'

'It's too far,' replied Stella. 'let's take them to our house. They'll be safe there and then we can come back for more.'

'We can't tell Grownups about us,' said Gus. 'They won't understand.'

'Mum and Dad will, Gus. Trust us, it's the only way we can save as many animals as possible.'

The little bird looked at Stella and knew she was right. 'Okay,' he said. 'Let's go.'

It was just after dawn when Stella and Dot walked into their parents' bedroom and gently woke them.

'What is it? What's wrong?' asked their mother.

'We're fine Mum, but some animals need your help,' Stella explained.

'Can't we bandage things later?' asked their father, half asleep. He presumed Stella was talking about her rabbit.

'No, Dad, this is serious.'

'Serious how, Stella? What is it, girls? You're scaring me.'

'We'll just have to show you, Mum.'

The girls led their parents to the back door and out into the garden. There on the lawn was the huge old ship containing thousands of cockatoos, koalas, echidnas, kookaburras, ring tailed possums, galahs, kangaroos, rainbow lorikeets, wallabies and so many more.

Stella watched her parents stare in disbelief.

Gus waddled towards them.

'Hello Mr and Mrs Peters. My name is Gus, it's a pleasure to meet you.'

Chapter Eight

Stella looked at her sister. 'Dad looked like he was going to faint when Gus talked to him.'

'Yeah,' said Dot, smiling but with tears in her eyes. It had been an emotional night already, and there was still so much work to do.

'How are you, Dot?' Dot nodded her head.

'What do you need me to do?'

'You're doing so well,' Stella said gently. 'How about you and Nelson get all the towels and sheets. I'll go get Dad.'

She found him in her parents' bedroom, hurriedly pulling his vet uniform on over his pyjamas. Stella got his vet bag for him and they moved towards the garden. Dot ran past them under a pile of sheets, Nelson following her with the Peters' towels. 'Sorry Dad,' said Dot as she knocked him out of the way. The frog gave him a wink.

'No worries!' said Mr Peters, laughing oddly. Stella joined him as he entered the garden. The sight of all the injured animals was shocking.

'Fill me in,' he said, going into vet mode.

'All the animals here are from the bushfires. We brought them to you on that ship so that we can go and get some more. The children are our friends. They've cleaned their wounds and bandaged them as best as they could. Mum and Gus are taking drinking water around.'

'Right, I'll start inspecting them. I'm going to need some pain killers and antibiotics. Here's the key to the clinic. You know what you're looking for.' The Peters' veterinary practice was attached to their house and Mr Peters had been teaching Stella for quite some time. She was an excellent student. 'We'll use the clinic for surgery and to treat smoke inhalation.'

The girls' parents moved around the garden, inspecting the patients while the girls helped.

Gus came to find them. 'The frogs and I are going to take the ship to get more animals now.'

'I'm coming too,' said Stella.

'No, you are not,' said her mother.

'Mum, I've already been on the ship remember. I've already saved lots of animals. I know what I'm doing.'

'There is no way you are getting on that thing without me.'

'Fine. You can come too then.'

'But, but…your father can't manage alone…'

'It's all right, Rosie, Dot and the children can help me with the surgery. You go with Stella. She's got this.'

Mrs Peters looked at her daughter's stubborn face. 'Fine, let's go.'

Stella and her mother ran over to the *Salvager*. The frogs had prepared the ship to leave and the balloon stood high. Stella held her mother's hand as she climbed down into the ship and it rose above the garden.

'Aren't there any seatbelts?' said her mother, who had started to mumble oddly to herself.

'No, Mum. Please stop being weird,' said Stella, who had enough to worry about.

Fauna ran up the plank. 'Can I come?' he asked. 'Please, Stella.'

'Jump on.'

The ship picked up speed and flew as fast as it could across the Australian countryside, farmers feeling a rush of wind as they started their morning's work but not seeing a thing. Soon they saw the fires on the horizon and Mrs Peters squeezed her daughter's hand. 'You will not put yourself in danger, Stella. That is an order.'

'Sure, Mum.'

Some of the frogs had stayed in the garden to help the patients so Stella, her mother and Fauna were needed on deck.

'Help me with the cannon please, Mum,' Stella shouted to her mother as the air started to fill with smoke.

'Cannon. Of course.'

Gus opened his mouth; a flame lit the cannon's wick and boom! the silvery bubble exploded into the air, once again growing bigger and bigger until it had surrounded the ship with a pop. Stella watched her mother shrug her shoulders; she was starting to get used to all of the extraordinary stuff.

The ship landed and Gus squelched through the wall to see who he could find.

'I'm going to help find some animals,' said Stella.

'No, no way,' said her mother.

'Mu—'

'Absolutely not Stella Peters, you are NOT allowed.' Stella recognized the look on her mother's face and knew it was pointless to argue.

'Fine. Fauna, help me get some more water and

bandages ready.'

Finally, Gus returned with a wingful of animals. Stella rushed to carry a joey kangaroo who could no longer stand up. 'Where are the rest?' she asked her friend but he just shook his head and looked up at her with tears in his eyes.

'They've all gone, Stella. We can't save them now.' Stella didn't want to believe it. She carried the joey down to the ship, and her mother and Fauna rushed to help. He was badly burnt and struggling to breathe.

'We need to get him home, Stella,' said her mother.

'But what about the others!' Stella couldn't hold the tears back. She searched her mother's face for an answer.

'The fires have taken them darling. There's nothing more we can do here.'

Stella ran to the side of the ship and plunged her head through the bubble. The heat on the other side immediately struck her face. She opened her eyes and saw nothing: the land was completely desolate. Her mother pulled her back in and she buried her face in her mother's uniform and cried.

Chapter Nine

Healesville, Victoria, 3 p.m.

It was quiet at the Peters' garden when the *Salvager* returned. Most of the animals were sleeping, River and Forest checking on their wounds and helping them to sip water when they needed it. Gus led the new injured animals to the makeshift beds the frogs had made and Stella and her mother carried the joey kangaroo to the clinic. Her father and Dot hadn't stopped and animals recovering from surgery filled the clinic. Some hadn't made it. Dot looked up at her sister, her eyes red from crying. They didn't have time to stop though, the family working together throughout the day until everyone had been treated.

That night the animals started to wake up and talk to one another. To Mr and Mrs Peters it sounded like feeding time at the zoo but to Stella and her friends it just sounded like lots of voices, all talking at once.

Gus flew up to the roof and said, 'Shhh, please everyone, quiet now so we can hear what everybody has to say.' But it didn't do much good, so the girls tried.

'Hello everyone!' tried Stella, with no luck.

'QUUIIEEETTTTT!!!' screamed Dot, who had always been able to make an incredible amount of noise, and the crowd went silent.

'Thank you,' she said, and sat down.

Stella cleared her throat. 'Thank you for trusting us and getting on the ship. It must have been terrifying and we're so sorry that you've lost your friends and family and homes. There's lots of bush around our house where Mum and Dad say you can go and live when you're better. Or, we want to tell you about another place, called Planet Beatrice.'

The crowd looked suspicious. A blue tongue lizard's tongue darted out of his mouth, a bilby hid under a leaf and a cockatoo squawked.

'What did she say?' asked a bandicoot.

'Planet Beatrice, you deaf coot,' replied his wife. 'Northern Territory.'

'Oh no, we're not moving to the NT,' said a platypus. 'Far too hot.'

'Beatrice is a planet, a lot like this one, but run by children, so there isn't any digging big holes, knocking trees down or making lots of smoke. It's not getting as hot there as it is here and no one starts bushfires. There's lots of room for you to go and live peacefully. If you would like to, we can take you in the ship.'

The animals started to talk amongst themselves and Stella sat down. After a little while a koala moved to the front of the crowd. 'I would like to speak,' she said.

The girls climbed down from the roof and knelt down in front of her. 'Please do,' said Stella 'It's Pella, isn't it?'

'Yes,' said the koala, 'and this is my joey, Nara. Thank you for saving my baby's life, I can never repay you. But a new planet...it's all very strange and frightening. Koalas have lived in Australia for millions of years. We pass on stories from our mothers to our joeys. My mother told me we have always faced danger. We were hunted for meat, and then for fur, but it's our home.'

'I understand,' said Stella. 'I was nervous to go too at first. But when I saw it, I fell in love with it, and I think you will as well.'

'Maybe,' replied Pella. 'Maybe now's the time. The danger is much greater than it's ever been before. So much of our habitat has been destroyed because of droughts and bushfires and to make new human homes. And then when we're forced to move closer to cities we're often killed by cats and dogs.'

The animals in the crowd murmured in agreement.

'Please, go on,' said Stella.

'Thank you. No one has ever listened before. We get our name from an Aboriginal term meaning 'no drink', as we get most of the moisture we need from eating the leaves of eucalyptus trees, but we do need to drink water as well. When we get too hot or can't get enough water we can die, so our home getting hotter and hotter is really bad for us.'

'We've studied it at school,' said Stella. 'We call it climate change.'

'But if humans know what it is, can't you stop it?'

'Some of us are trying, but it's not enough.'

Pella paused to think. 'So, there are eucalyptus trees on Planet Beatrice? And water?'

'Yes,' said Gus. 'There's a land on the planet that is just like your bush, but untouched and safe.'

'There are children there like us, they care about you. They call the planet, Bea. Can we at least show you, Pella?' said Dot. 'If you don't like it, you can come back here and find a new home on Earth.'

Nara looked up at her mother. 'Okay,' said Pella. 'Show

us.' And the brave little koala smiled.

The next day the animals that wanted to leave, and were well enough to go, boarded the ship. Insects, animals and birds marched, hopped and flew up into the ship as Stella and the children helped them settle in for the journey.

The Peters family had discussed everything and it was decided that Mr and Mrs Peters would stay and look after the animals in the clinic.

'Please be careful,' said Mrs Peters to the girls.

'We will, Mum,' said Stella. 'Bea is a lovely place. Nothing bad happens there. Except when you're playing Leap Frog, but don't worry about that.'

'What?'

'They'll be fine, Rosie, they're smart girls,' said Mr Peters, and he held his wife.

'Back for school please!' shouted their mother, blotting tears from her eyes as they boarded the ship.

Gus lit the wick and up went the balloon, all dusky golds, pinks and reds to match the setting sun.

The frogs started to sing and everyone felt a mixture of sadness and relief. Stella went into the hold of the ship to look for blankets. She watched Gus jump up onto a bed and close his eyes. He looked very tired. She sat next to him and stroked his feathers. One eye gently opened to see who it was and then he smiled. 'You're a good girl, Stella. I'm so proud of you.' Stella stayed until the sound of soft snoring came from the little bird. She found the blankets in a cupboard, wrapped one around him and carried the rest out onto the deck.

She saw some short-beaked echidnas huddling in a corner. 'How are you? OK?' she asked.

'Yes!' said one laughing loudly, and a bit nervously. 'Oh yes yes, yes. No. No probably not. I'm sorry, I'm just not myself today. I mean I'm normally verrry busy you know, lots of ants to find, ground to cover et cetera, et cetera. Leave no stone unturned, haha! Just umm, don't have any food right now.' He fell silent.

'Oh, I'm so sorry! What is it you eat? Ants?'

'Ants, termites, the odd beetle, lavae. Anything little really, has to fit in my mouth you see. Not so big my mouth. But my sense of smell is second to none! Lots of smells on this ship, goodness me! Not so many ants.'

'Well, I have it on good authority that there will be millions of them when we get to Bea. Can you hold on?'

'Oh yes! Survivors us echidnas. Oldest surviving mammals in the world don't you know. Seventeen million years! Take more than that bushfire to kill old Admiral, haha.'

'Hi Admiral, it's a pleasure to meet you.' Stella smiled.

'Oh yes, you too, you too, dear girl. Phenomenal rescuing, well done. I mean normally it's safer for us to stay where we are in bushfires so that foxes don't find us. We can hide in the ash from the fire you see, lower our body temperature and not move around so much so that we don't need as much food and energy. But I suppose this climate change is making bigger and fiercer fires which means fewer places for us to hide.'

'We lived through a smaller bushfire last year,' said a bush rat. His nose twitched nervously and he kept looking over his shoulder at a copperhead snake. 'We decided to stay where we were and not make a run for it. We found a wombat burrow and hid in it until the fire passed.'

'You're very brave,' said Stella. 'And you don't have anything to worry about on this ship, do you friend?' She was looking at the copperhead. He lowered his head.

'Sssssssure, nothing to worry about on this sssshhhhip.' Stella arched her eyebrow. 'I promisssse!' the snake tutted and fell asleep.

'Here,' said Stella to the echidnas and bush rat, making beds for them out of the blankets. 'Everything's going to be all right.' The group snuggled together, and Stella continued to walk around the ship. A crowd had gathered and she nestled her way to River, Fauna and Forest at the front.

'You've got to see this,' said River, laughing.

Dot had drawn a hopscotch grid on the floor and Nelson and the other frogs were jumping all over it.

'No.' Dot was instructing the frogs. 'So you throw the stone on the first square and then hop over it and keep hopping until you reach the end and then you hop back, pick up the stone and don't hop on that square.'

Nelson threw the stone onto the square, hopped on top of it and then all the frogs piled on top of him trying to get the stone.

'I don't think you understand the rules,' said Dot, separating the army of frogs.

Stella smiled and kept going. Ahead a kookaburra had flown onto a post, up on the mast. Beneath him sat young members of the ship's passengers.

'Now,' lectured the bird, 'who knows which kingfisher is the largest of the kingfishers?'

The young animals were silent.

'The kookaburra! Oh, deary me, don't know who the largest is.' A collared kingfisher rolled her eyes.

'And do you know that when we mate it's for life! Absolutely, very dedicated parents we are, isn't that right, Colin?' The kookaburra motioned down to his son and the young kookaburra nodded with embarrassment.

'Yes, Dad.'

'Of course, many people know us for our laugh…' the kookaburra cleared his throat and let out an enormous cackle, waking up anyone asleep on the ship. 'There's even a song about it,' he said proudly. 'Now, who knows why we laugh?'

'Someone's told a joke?' asked a young possum.

'No!' replied the kookaburra. 'Common mistake that. No, it's not really a laugh you see, it's a way of saying this is our place to the other kookaburras.'

'What happened to the other kookaburras in the fire?' asked one of the possums.

The kookaburra looked into the distance. His voice became quieter. 'Many of our kind will have been killed or injured. The birds that are left behind will be in shock and at risk from other animals. Those that survive will have to wait for new plants to grow and, in time, insects and animals will return. You see, when there's a bushfire the whole ecosystem is damaged.'

'What's an ecosystem?' asked a joey.

'It's an area where plants and animals as well as the weather and landscape work together to form a bubble of life.'

Stella thought about the bush and how long it would take to recover. The kookaburra regained his composure. 'Right, who wants to play a game?'

The young group shouted, 'Me!'

'Excellent. It's called 'who knows the most about

kookaburras?"'

The students groaned. Stella smiled and left them to it.

She walked over to the edge of the ship and looked out at space. It was so big. Her town seemed tiny now. It was hard to take in all that she'd been through recently. Right now, all she wanted was to get the animals to Bea safely and go home. She felt tears in her eyes.

'Are you all right, dear?' Stella jumped; a kangaroo stood next to her. She was taller than Stella and looked incredibly strong. 'You look like you need a cuddle.' And the kangaroo pulled her close. Stella nuzzled into the kangaroo's warm fur and instantly felt better.

'Thanks,' she said.

'I'm Martha,' said the kangaroo.

'I'm Stella.'

'Ooh, I know who you are love, I think everyone does. Bit of a hero, I'd say.'

'I'm not a hero. I've been scared a lot.'

'That doesn't matter. Being scared is normal. Be a bit odd if you didn't get scared.'

'I think Mum and Dad would be better at this than me.'

'Maybe love, but adults get scared too. I'm a Mum and I'm still terrified a lot of the time. In fact, it's scarier when you've got young. You're more worried about them than you are yourself.'

'Are your joeys safe?' Stella was scared again, scared to hear the answer.

'They are dear, thanks to you and your friends. We went back through the fire to where the land had burnt. We knew it couldn't burn again. That's where you found us. Didn't get away completely though…' Martha turned and looked at her tail. The fur on her back was singed and her tail bandaged, the wounds weeping.

Stella breathed in sharply. It looked very painful. 'Oh Martha. Come on, let's get something for the pain and change those bandages.'

Stella took Martha's paw and started to lead the way. 'Look!' Martha pointed to a shooting star as it zipped past the balloon. 'Let's make a wish.' They closed their eyes and wished that somehow other animals had managed to survive the fires.

Chapter Ten

The small planet came into view and everyone scrambled to see it. It looked just like Earth had done as they left, but smaller.

All the passengers clambered to the sides of the ship to see their new home.

'Don't move around too much please,' said Gus. 'We're just dropping River, Forest and Fauna off.'

The ship hovered over the treehouse and everyone ran out to see it.

'There's Flora, and Bramble!'

'Looks like you've got a full load! Well done!' shouted Flora.

'Thanks. We'll be back soon,' said Stella. 'There's so much I want to talk to you about.'

'I can't wait to catch up. Come and see me when you're not so busy!'

River joined Stella. 'You've done so well. Look how many animals you've saved!' he looked around at the packed ship.

'I wish I could have saved them all,' said Stella.

'You did better than anyone else could have. You're amazing.' Stella wasn't great at taking compliments but she made herself look up.

'Thanks, River, I'll see you soon.'

'Looking forward to it,' said River taking a big bow. He

picked up the rope and climbed over the side of the ship, they smiled at each other and he jumped off and down to the treehouse.

Stella turned to Forest. 'Bye Forest.'

'Bye, Stella, I'm proud of you.' Forest raised her hand and Stella put hers against it.

'Bye, Stella,' said Fauna.

'Bye, Fauna, good job.'

'You too.' He picked up his rope. 'Looking forward to kicking your bum in Leap Frog!' He laughed and jumped off the ship.

'Can't wait!' said Stella rolling her eyes.

The ship rose high above the treehouse with all on the deck waving and cheering at the sisters and the saved animals. The *Salvager* picked up speed towards Bea's bushland, the animals studying the landscape as it flew past. After a little while the ship started to slow.

'Excuse me everyone, we're here,' announced Gus, 'please start carefully making your way off the ship.'

The girls helped everyone onto the plank and a long line of animals started to set foot on a brand-new planet.

Some king parrots flew onto the branches of a tree; snakes slithered into holes in the ground and some wallabies looked around some caves. Everyone was keen to explore. Dot carried a young possum from the ship and tried to put her down on the ground but the possum clung to her like a baby.

'Don't worry, I'll stay with you.' Dot sat on the ground and the possum curled up in her lap.

Stella carried a bucket of fish to the stream where she and River had collected water the last time they were there.

'Welcome to your new home!' Stella said to the fish, and they swam around and around the bucket with excitement. She tipped them into the crisp water. A murray cod swam to the surface and said, 'This place is beaut! Thanks Stella!' then flicked his tail and swam off up the stream.

Stella stood still for a moment, breathing everything in. It was a moment she wanted to remember forever.

Back at the camp everyone had made their way off the ship. Stella walked up to Gus, 'How is everybody?' she asked.

'Excellent, they all love it!' he replied.

'I'm so glad.'

Dot came towards them, still carrying her possum. 'I don't want to leave.'

'We have to go home, Dot. They'll all be safe here. Who's this?' Stella stroked the possum.

'Zellie. She lost her mum in the fire.'

'Oh, Zellie. Would you like to stay here or come home with me and Dot?'

'I want to stay with Dot,' squeaked Zellie. Dot smiled and stroked her head.

'No problem. Come home with us then.' Stella patted her sister on the back.

'Can you get everyone's attention please Dot?' she asked her sister. 'Without terrifying the living daylights out of us?' she added.

Dot covered the possum's ears. 'EVERYONE LISTEN UP!' she yelled. Stella let out an exasperated sigh.

'Sorry, everyone,' announced Stella. 'Please have a look around, we hope you like it. If anyone wants to come back with us to Australia, you're very welcome, we'll be leaving soon. We just really hope that if you do decide to stay that you'll be happy here. We know you'll be safe.'

Pella and Nara the koalas walked over to them. 'We've decided to stay,' said Pella.

'That's great news, Pella! I'm excited for your new beginnings.' Stella hugged the mother and daughter koalas.

'Me too,' said the mother.

'We're also going to stay,' said Admiral, his fellow echidnas sniffing the air.

'Wonderful, Admiral. You take care.' Stella stroked the echidna's little beak.

'Oh yes, yes, yes, absolutely my dear. Thank you. I shall think of you every time I find a nice colony of ants.'

'We'll stay, too,' said Martha, her two joeys hopping happily in the sun.

'Martha!' Stella was fighting back tears now. 'How is your tail?'

'It'll be just fine, love. Thank you.'

All the animals took it in turns to hug their human friends.

'We will come back won't we, Gus?' asked Dot, wiping her face on her t-shirt.

'Absolutely, little miss, we'll come and check on them soon.'

The animals waved goodbye and hopped, shuffled and flew into the bush.

Stella and Dot and Dot's new possum, Zellie, climbed up to the crow's nest of the ship and watched as the morning sun rose over the planet.

'Now, I believe you two girls are required at school

today?' chirped Gus. The girls groaned.

'What about if we go and see a friend of mine on the way first?' he added with a twinkle in his eye.

'Yay!' shouted the girls.

'To the ocean please, frogs. Let's find Daisy!'

The *Salvager* picked up speed and rushed over trees and then fields and then there on the horizon was a great glimmer of shimmering blue. 'I see the sea!' shouted Dot.

'Me too!' said Stella. 'Who is Daisy!'

'Daisy,' said Gus, 'is a Steller's sea cow.'

'A sea cow?' asked Dot. 'Cows can't swim!'

'This one can,' said Gus, and the ship began to slow as it passed over a long stretch of sandy beach, and then over the ocean. The sun's early morning rays cast a *Salvager*-shaped shadow over the shallow waters.

'Who's that stealing my morning sun?' asked a toothless mouth and hairy nose popping out of the water.

'Only me, Daisy!' said Gus.

A huge, black, blubbery seal-like body could just be seen under the water as Daisy moved towards the ship to greet her friend.

'Gus!' she said. 'And new friends I see.'

'Daisy, I would like to introduce you to Stella and Dot. They have been an enormous help saving some animals from Earth this week.'

'A pleasure to meet you, girls!' said the Steller's sea cow, munching on some kelp.

'And you!' replied Stella, taking in Daisy's whale-like tail.

'Where are you off to?' asked Daisy.

'School unfortunately,'

'School,' pondered Daisy. 'Like a school of fish?'

'I know this!' said Dot. 'A school of fish is when a group of fish swim together in the same direction!'

'It is!' said Daisy. 'Are you swimming today?'

'No, I think we've got netball,' replied Dot.

'No idea what that is my dear, but I do hope it's fun. Well then, until next time girls!' said Daisy, and the steller's sea cow slowly moved her massive body under the water in search of more kelp.

'Bye Daisy!' chorused the girls.

'She was lovely. Has she always lived here, or did you bring her?' Dot asked Gus.

'I brought Daisy's great grandmother and some of her friends here 260 years ago. The last of their kind, terribly sadly.'

'What happened to the rest of her family?'

'They were all killed by hunters, I'm sorry to say. All in the seventeen years after humans discovered them.'

The girls couldn't believe people could wipe out an entire species so quickly.

'But Gus saved them,' Stella said to her little sister, putting her arm around her and cheering her up. 'And we're going to save lots more animals.'

'Yes,' said Dot. 'I can't wait.'

'I shall be back in a week for our next mission,' said Gus. 'I thought we would start in Central Asia: there are some snow leopards that need our help. But first, school!' said Gus. 'To Earth, froggies! And as quick as you can!'

The girls held on to the bow of the ship as it gathered speed over the ocean, water spraying them and making them squeal with delight. The sky was a glorious gold, peach and blue as the sun rose over Planet Beatrice. Breeds of birds they had never seen before flew alongside the hot air balloon whose pattern had changed to a school of fish, diving up and down and around the balloon's lining. Up the balloon soared towards space.

'See you soon, Bea!' sang the girls at the top of their lungs.

Printed in Australia
Ingram Content Group Australia Pty Ltd
AUHW020602251023
385505AU00001B/2

9 781804 391747